Little Black Dress

Little Black Dress

A Peter Macklin Novel of Suspense

Loren D. Estleman

This Large Print edition is published by Wheeler Publishing, Waterville, Maine USA and by BBC Audiobooks, Ltd, Bath, England.

Published in 2005 in the U.S. by arrangement with St. Martin's Press, LLC.

Published in 2005 in the U.K. by arrangement with St. Martin's Press.

U.S. Hardcover 1-59722-006-X (Compass)
U.K. Hardcover 1-4056-3414-6 (Chivers Large Print)

A Peter Macklin Novel of Suspense

This is a work of fiction. All the characters and events portrayed in this novel are either fictitious or are used fictitiously.

The text of this Large Print edition is unabridged.
Other aspects of the book may vary from the original edition.

Set in 16 pt. Plantin by Ramona Watson.

Printed in the United States on permanent paper.

British Library Cataloguing-in-Publication Data available

Library of Congress Cataloging-in-Publication Data

Estleman, Loren D.
Little black dress : a Peter Macklin mystery / by Loren D. Estleman.
p. cm. — (Wheeler Publishing large print compass)
ISBN 1-59722-006-X (lg. print : hc : alk. paper)
1. Macklin, Peter (Fictitious character) — Fiction. 2. Murder for hire — Fiction. 3. Mothers-in-law — Fiction. 4. Married people — Fiction. 5. Retirees — Fiction. 6. Robbery — Fiction. 7. Large type books. 8. Ohio — Fiction. I. Title. II. Wheeler large print compass series.
PS3555.S84L58 2005b
813′.54—dc22 2005007300

For Jim O'Keefe,
a kind friend in the mean streets

ONE

It was always a mistake to generalize; but, dear God, security guards were dumb.

Grinnell spotted him two steps inside the door, browsing the Japanese Animation racks in a Hawaiian shirt with the tail out over his sidearm, khaki slacks, and clod-buster black oxfords, the kind whose soles formed a lip all around with white stitching to make the feet that wore them look even bigger. He never stooped even once to look at the videos on the lower shelves, saving his energy to pretend to read the descriptions on the boxes he took off the top. He wore a bar of black moustache as thick as his thumb and his hair looked as if he cut it himself. He might as well have been wearing a uniform.

The layout was identical to all the other stores in the chain, a case man's dream. It had separate doors for entering and exiting, the latter charged with a magnetic field to set off an alarm when a customer tried to sneak *Free Willy* out unchecked, and a blind room in back where they displayed the porn. Two employees stood inside the hollow square of the counter while a third restocked the racks, carefully avoiding conversation with the security lunk. Midnight closing was ten minutes away and only a few customers prowled the store. The locustlike Saturday-night crowd had swept through more than two hours earlier, scooping up New Releases by the armload and cracking twenties and fifties into two cash registers. Now the gold dust had settled. Even the monitors narrowcasting annoying trailers for Adam Sandler and Austin Powers were switched off.

Showtime.

Grinnell made a little dumb show of exasperation at the shelves of empty boxes that had contained the latest hot-ticket title, then left, answering a curious glance from the clerk nearest the door with a rueful shake of his head.

The minivan was parked on the far edge of the lot, just outside the range of the near lamppost. The man in the passenger's seat in front rolled down his window as Grinnell approached. The man wore his sandy hair long but neat, with a drooping gunfighter's moustache stained yellow at the edges from nicotine. Grinnell supposed he dipped snuff, the most pointless abuse of tobacco he could imagine.

"Three clerks," Grinnell said. "One guard." He described the man in the Hawaiian shirt.

"Anything there?" The man in the van had a Kentucky accent that he could dial up or down according to mood. Grinnell couldn't tell if it was genuine. The other three men in the vehicle called him Wild Bill.

"Not to look at, but you want to pin him down first. This is the fourth time for this chain." It was a warning, but he stopped short of making it a suggestion. He hadn't had any trouble with this crew, but it was never wise to underestimate the sensitivity of a wrecker, much less of one who allowed his team to address him by an Old West nickname.

"What else?"

"The clerk stocking the racks wears a nose ring; tattoos on both wrists. He might be a user."

"What else?" he asked again.

"That's it."

"Okay." The window slid back up.

The parking lot was common to eight shops assembled in a strip, occupying one long building with only drywall separating each establishment from its neighbor. Grinnell had parked a hundred yards away, near a number of vehicles in front of a twenty-four-hour drugstore. The car was a rental, not his usual choice of models when he wasn't working, a deliberate decision. He never used his personal car on a job and always took care to dress suitably for the community. The video store stood within easy walking distance of two trailer parks and a housing tract designed for families of modest means; he wore a plain pocket T-shirt, faded Lee jeans, and inexpensive track shoes worn round at the heels.

He drove a mile to the crowded motel lot where he'd left his Lexus, changed inside it into his comfortable heavy silk sport shirt, pleated slacks, and Belgian loafers, and drove the Lexus home. In the morning he'd return the rental. The agency was only twelve blocks away, comfortable walking for a fortyish man in excellent condition.

"What do we need him for, anyway? I guess I can count noses and spot a rent-a-cop."

Wild Bill glanced back at the speaker. His features were in shadow, but Carlos always sat in the same place, as if the seat were assigned to him, and if there was a complaint to be made he was always the one to make it. Then there was the bullshit macho border accent. Wild Bill was pretty sure he was East L.A. and had never spent any more time in Old Mexico than forty-five minutes in a cockshop in Tijuana.

"It ain't them he's watching," Wild Bill said. "Toledo protects its investments."

"What investment? Guns are cheap."

"Not these guns." The man in front lifted the shotgun from his lap and worked the pump. It slid noiselessly on graphite and chambered the round with a double clack he felt in his testicles. The weapon was less than twenty-two inches long, manufactured that way without recourse to a hacksaw, with a composition stock and a pistol grip. It was loaded alternately with twelve-gauge slugs and buckshot. He always used the same order so he knew what was coming out of the barrel when. He'd learned that hunting elk in Wyoming.

"Yeah." Carlos's grin reflected what light there was. He was looking down at the Sig Sauer in his hand, a cop gun he'd turned out to prefer to the Saturday-night busters he'd used in his solo past. It took a little more persuasion each time to get him to part with the model between jobs.

"Then there's the credit-card slips," Wild Bill said. "Folks're using plastic more and more. We can't lay them off in a year."

"Fucking Visa's ruining the economy," Carlos said.

The other man shifted his line of vision. "Mark?"

The man seated next to Carlos in the rear passenger's seat waggled his own Sig Sauer to indicate he was ready. He was black, a Detroit native with back-to-back nickel bits in Michigan's two state penitentiaries on his record, whose given name — Wild Bill had seen his arrest sheet to confirm it — was Mark Twain. During one of his rare open moments (on parrot tranquilizers) he'd confided that his father was drunk when he'd named him, having smuggled a fifth of Ten High into a movie theater in suburban Redford to celebrate his son's birth. The feature happened to be *Tom Sawyer.* In the time he'd known him, Wild Bill had never heard Mark Twain say anything remotely clever, but he had eloquent instincts. When the time came to talk Carlos out of his weapon, it would be Mark Twain who did the talking.

"Take it slow," Wild Bill said.

The driver turned the key and rolled the

van out of its space. Prematurely bald, he cropped the fringe to the length of his perennial three-day beard and answered to Donny. Wild Bill knew nothing about him except that he'd come with Mark Twain, who said he'd worked as an instructor with a driving school in Kentucky that taught evasive skills to chauffeurs of wealthy businessmen. So far he'd only been called upon to deliver his companions to and away from work, without having to demonstrate special abilities. He was always there when they came out, which made him worth his equal share if he never took another risk.

As they wheeled into the fire lane in front of the video store, Wild Bill leaned forward and spat the rest of his cud into the coffee can. He gave himself a moment to enjoy his personal vision of success. Bank robbers were lucky if they got away with a couple of thousand from a teller's drawer, for which they had the opportunity when caught to be tried twice, at the local and federal levels, and get themselves butt-fucked by an entirely different class of con. Meanwhile a place that rented out videotapes and DVDs in a greater metropolitan area pulled in eight to ten thousand on a Saturday night, most of it cash, with nothing to protect it but civilian security more interested in shoplifters than armed robbers. Hit them just before midnight, when the suburban cops were busy changing shifts, and you could take the rest of the month off. Hooray for Hollywood.

Emily Grass, checking the last of a thousand returned videos against the labels on the cases, suppressed a groan when the gong went off announcing the entrance of a new customer. It was three minutes to twelve, and you just knew this was some trailer-park 'tard who couldn't remember the title of the movie he'd come in for, or didn't know what he wanted, *Cannonball Run* or *Faces of Death IV*, and would wander the aisles for twenty minutes looking for inspiration. Worse, he might ask her to identify a movie based on a cast headed by Whatsername, that played the lady lawyer in Whateveritwascalled, breathing Old Milwaukee into her face the whole time and not budging from the counter even if you turned out all the lights. Which Cy would never let her do because he might squeeze three more bucks out of the night and put himself in solid with the corporate blanks that owned the chain. Come next term break, she'd find something in retail foods. Those supermarket managers shoved you out the door at closing and dropped a piano on overtime.

Then she saw the ski masks.

All three were dressed the same, in the navy masks and green polo shirts with an animal on the pocket, black jeans, and black Nikes; she saw the swoosh. The first one in the door, who did most of the yelling, made big circular gestures with a rifle kind of gun while the others separated, one pointing his handgun at the three customers lined up at the counter, the other pointing his at Andy the guard, who was caught looking at *Inspector Gadget* and dropped the box to put his hands up. The one with the rifle, or maybe it was a shotgun, hoisted it to his shoulder and shouted at Michael, coming back for more videos to return to the shelves, to join the others at the counter. He obeyed, hands lifted with the blue FOREVER DEAD and GARCIA LIVES tattoos showing on his wrists. Then the man stood back to cover — *cover*, she'd seen enough crime trailers to speak the language — cover them all while he screamed at Emily and Dylan to empty the registers into bags. Emily got her drawer open okay, but Dylan hit two keys at once, jamming the electronics, and got yelled at some more until he cleared it, sobbing, "Okayokayokayokay." And all the time there she was, stuffing stacks of bills and fistfuls of credit-card slips into a white plastic bag with the chain's logo printed on it, a cartoon squirrel rolling a reel of film like a hoop. It was a movie.

Then it wasn't at all.

Cy came charging out of the room where they stocked the dirty pictures, fat Cy in his black indestructible manager's suit and Tweety Bird tie, waving a gun. Cy with a gun; he couldn't reprogram the VCRs after a power failure put out the clocks. Cy with a gun, shouting at three men, also with guns, that they were under citizen's arrest, drop your weapons and stand back. He ran right past the man covering Andy, heading straight for the man with the shotgun, who just kind of turned half away from the counter and blew all the sound out of the room.

TWO

"Look, they poured a floor," Laurie said. "This used to be a Michigan basement."

Macklin sniffed the dank cellar air. "I thought we were in Ohio."

"You know what a Michigan basement is. It was just a hole in the dirt, and it smelled like potatoes. The bin used to be in that corner. I reached in once to get a big baker and grabbed hold of a rat."

"Good thing it was a dirt floor. You'd have had a mess to clean up."

"I screamed, all right, but I'd had worse scares. Old Nick chased me clear to the fence once. I've still got a scar on my ankle from scrambling over the barbed wire."

"I wondered about that. Old Nick was the idiot farmhand?"

"*I* was the idiot farmhand. Old Nick was an Angus bull, mean as a snake. I knew better than to take the shortcut. Papa Z spanked me but good when he found out. He was more scared than I was."

"How'd he find out?"

"I told him."

"You're right. You were an idiot."

She found a second switch at the base of the stairs and flipped it. A second set of track lights illuminated the rest of the basement. The current owners had laid rusty shag on the concrete and paneled the walls in particleboard with a maple veneer. A small bar with two stools stood in front of the partitioned-off utility room and four craters showed in the carpet where a pool or Ping-Pong table had stood until recently. A plaid sofa and love seat and some chairs, probably belonging to a living-room set demoted to the rec room, had a neglected look. The bar hadn't been used in a long time. The cellar had begun to reclaim itself. The atmosphere was mildewy and spots of white mold showed on the paneling on the north wall.

"How long did your grandfather own the place?" Macklin asked.

"Fifty years, until his stroke. Mama Z was gone by then and Mother put him in a nursing home." Laurie grinned. "Are you nervous about meeting Mother?"

"I met her at the wedding."

"That doesn't count. Everyone has to be nice at a wedding."

"A woman my age, whose daughter I stole? Why worry?"

She shook her head. "I never can predict you. My friends said I shouldn't marry you because you had no sense of humor."

Macklin walked to the end of the basement and paced off its length. It came to sixty feet, the length of the house minus the garage that had been built on within the last ten years. He looked up at the exposed joists. "I wonder what it would cost to install a soundproof ceiling."

"Why?"

"I might put in a workshop. I wouldn't want to disturb you with power tools some night while you're watching TV."

"Why do you need a shooting range? You told me you were retired."

He smiled, without amusement. Her fresh, pretty face and unclouded blue eyes made him forget sometimes how quickly her mind worked. Her mouth was tense.

"My enemies aren't," he said. "I need to hit the bull's-eye every time."

Peter and Laurie Macklin had been married almost a year, and it had been a time of learning for them both: for him, that she was capable of things no one else suspected, including herself; for her, that the quiet, somewhat dull man she'd chosen to wed was a killer. Or had been a killer. Maybe it was a once-and-always thing, like a former chief of state still being addressed as President years after he'd left office.

Or maybe not. Because that would make her a killer too.

They went back upstairs and revisited the half-empty rooms on the ground floor. The atmosphere had changed since they'd gone to the basement. Earlier, she'd run from room to room like a little girl, showing him where Mama Z's huge six-burner range had stood in the kitchen, describing the heavy mahogany table in the dining room, the one that had come over from Germany with Mama Z's grandmother, the parlor used only by company and Papa Z, who employed it evenings as a den, smoking his bent-stem pipe and reading Karl May. On the second floor, she'd opened the door of her old room and told Peter, drawing him inside, that no man had ever been allowed to cross that threshold in her tender years. They'd kissed, and if there had been a full-size bed in the room instead of a child's twin, they might have had to scramble for discarded clothing when the real-estate agent came looking for them.

Now things were different, and all because of a question about a soundproof ceiling.

The agent, a tall, big-shouldered woman whose dyed black hair made her face look even harder, sensed immediately that they had had some kind of fight. Laurie could feel her apprehension. The woman stood holding her handbag in front of her, trying to blend into the hideous contemporary wallpaper. Most newlywed couples wanted to build, or buy new. Old farmhouses were a drug on the market, and there was just enough wetland in the eighty acres that accompanied this one to discourage developers. Laurie's mother had once sold real estate, and she herself had waded through every swampy inch at one time or another; she knew the value as well as anyone. The family that had bought the property from her grandfather's estate had placed most of their things in storage and moved in with relatives, leaving behind the desolate air of a house that had grown stale in the listings. The longer a realtor remained saddled with a white elephant, the more the stigma was likely to affect her career. Squabbling customers were not good prospects.

Laurie took pity on her. She gazed out the window at the emerald planting beyond the barn. “Who put in the corn?”

“A local farmer. The owners lease out twenty acres to keep it from becoming overgrown with brush.” The agent’s voice regained its professional chirp. “The rent goes a long way toward paying the taxes.”

“It ought to. He should trim those marijuana plants when they start sticking up above the stalks.”

The realtor reddened furiously. Peter laughed, loudly and unguardedly, surprising Laurie for the second time that day. She knew then they were okay. They were a newlywed couple like every other, still feeling their way about and marking the sore spots to avoid. Later she’d surprise him in turn by suggesting he put his firing range in the barn. She’d decided to buy the farm where she’d spent all her summers as a girl.

Edgar Prine, the captain in charge of the longest surviving task force in the history of the Ohio State Police, took armed robbery as a personal affront to his theory of an orderly universe. Insofar as he was a religious man, he believed God had hung the planets where he had according to a prearrangement that Man could never hope to understand, and that any attempt to alter their orbits was either doomed to fail or programmed to succeed by a system that had been in place billions of years before the first man-made rocket pierced the gravity belt. Haring about commercial districts with ski masks and guns was not part of the plan and it was his responsibility to discourage it even unto death. He'd gone about muttering this phrase — *even unto death* — for so long that men above and below him had taken to calling him "the Reverend Ed Prine," and not always behind his back. When this happened to his face, he glared, but he didn't protest. The task force's record of arrests that stuck was defense sufficient.

He was taller than he looked and bigger than he seemed. The width of his torso (he wore a size 54 jacket) impressed others more horizontally than vertically, and he was built in proportion so that his size didn't assert itself until those who met him for the first time were standing in the chill of his shadow. He was fifty years old but looked older, with a crease on each side of his face from eye pouch to jawline and white eyebrows that stood out like feelers. When he wore his uniform, at departmental funerals and other dress occasions, he looked like an admiral of the fleet, but in plainclothes suit and tie he could be mistaken for the president of a middling prosperous small-town bank. He had killed four men in the line of duty before he made sergeant and had survived one governor's attempt to dismiss him for misuse of deadly force.

A female television reporter in a tailored suit spotted him on his way across the parking lot, snatched her microphone out of the face of the man she was interviewing, and came his way, trailing her cameraman and a bearded hippie with a bank of lights on wheels. Prine didn't break stride. The woman fell off her heels, straight into the light man, whose lights tipped over, forcing him to lunge to save them from shattering against the asphalt. The cameraman avoided the domino effect with a Michael Jackson moonwalk and swung the lens to follow the police captain as he entered the video store. For the next two days, every time Prine turned on a TV set, he saw the same footage of his right shoulder and the back of his head going through the door. He placed the media on a level with satellites whizzing aimlessly among the fixed planets.

He summoned a city uniform from the crowd inside the store. The sergeant identified himself as the first officer on the scene and escorted him to the aisle where a little fat man lay spread-eagled on the floor with a nickel-plated Ruger lying just beyond the fingers of his right hand and all of the middle of him stamped flat as if by a giant shoe. Blood and bits of entrail radiated out from the body on both sides, making a visceral snowflake on the carpet.

"Cyrus Oliver, the manager." The city cop read from a spiral notebook. "Came running out of the triple-X-rated section holding the 9mm. No one knows if he had a permit. Ran into a load of double-O buck. One of the cashiers said the man with the shotgun had long blonde hair. Saw it sticking out from under the back of his mask." He pointed to a thin young woman talking to some other people near the counter. She was a college type with a punk cut and four-alarm acne.

"That fits with the description we got from two of the other holdups," Prine said. "What about the vehicle?"

"Minivan, blue or silver. We got that from the kid with the tattoos."

The captain followed the sergeant's pencil. The kid looked like a druggie. Okay if it was coke or some other upper, every eyewitness ought to indulge. "Model?"

"Says they all look alike. Which they do. This a state case, Captain?"

"I can't answer that question till your chief asks it. He coming?"

"Probably. We don't get many killings in Hilliard."

"What about the guard?"

The sergeant pointed him out, talking to another uniform. He hadn't really needed to. The man's sidearm made his Hawaiian shirt stick out in back. He might as well have been picking his nose with it.

"He at least draw his piece?"

"He says. Never got off a shot. The manager almost fell over him. They moved fast after that, scooped up what the cashier put in the bag and cleared out. The only experience most of these securities have is frisking shoplifters."

"Maybe he didn't *want* to get off a shot."

The sergeant nodded, as if he'd thought of that, and maybe he had. "Could be an inside job. An outfit like this usually has some kind of advance man, though, and nobody saw him talking to anyone."

"You know a lot about this kind of operation for someone who doesn't get much of it."

"Heists we get: convenience stores, and maybe twice a year a bank. We haven't had anybody killed in a couple of years."

"What's the cashier's name?" Prine asked.

The sergeant turned a page. "Emily Grass. She's a sophomore at State. This is a summer job."

That was useless information, but he stopped short of criticizing an officer he didn't command. The man was eager for a boost. "I'll talk to her."

"Want me to take notes?"

"No. Some people clam up when you start writing it down."

The cashier looked drawn. She might have been just tired. It was almost three o'clock, and in his time Prine had seen citizens' reactions to violence change. He supposed she and the others screened *From Dusk Till Dawn* after the customers left. Hollywood was getting it all these days. All but the smell, and in another couple of years the multiplexes would probably start pumping blood and excrement into the ventilator system during the action scenes.

"Ms. Grass?"

She nodded. She was breathing shallowly, shuddering on the exhale. Maybe she preferred Merchant-Ivory films. He asked if any strangers had been in that evening. She was a good observer, and after they put behind them the usual sass about most of the customers being strange, he had a pretty good description of the advance man. And he knew before laying eyes on the local chief of police that it was a state case.

Wild Bill answered the door holding a folded *USA Today*, one of the complimentary issues from the motel office. Grinnell knew what was inside it and that it would be one of the Sig Sauers from Toledo. The man was in his undershirt. The green polo shirt he'd worn earlier was flung across the room's only armchair and Grinnell knew it was covering the bag from the video store. Wild Bill got out of the way of the door and when it was closed he threw aside the newspaper and took the automatic off cock.

"What happened?" Grinnell asked.

"Character came out of the dirty-movie section waving a piece. Did you even go back there?"

"I looked inside. I thought he was a customer."

"Kind of careless."

Grinnell let it go. It wasn't anything he hadn't been thinking. "Where are the others?"

"We don't shack up together."

"What about the rest of the weapons?"

"In the closet." Wild Bill did a border roll and handed him the Sig Sauer. "Carlos didn't want to give this up."

"He going to be a problem?"

"Not as long as Mark Twain's around." He threw the polo shirt onto the bed. The cash was in a pile with the credit-card slips stacked neatly next to it.

Grinnell split the stack in two and put a sheaf in each pocket of his nylon windbreaker. Then he went to the built-in closet and hoisted the duffel he found there off the floor. The shotgun was the heaviest thing inside. "Anyone else open fire?"

"No."

"You'll get the same pistols back, then. Shotguns usually can't be identified by Ballistics, but things are changing by the day."

"Pretty soon we got to start reading *Police Times* just to keep up."

Grinnell zipped open the duffel and put the Sig Sauer inside. "Take a month off."

"Not till I get my stake."

Grinnell didn't ask. It was bad enough he'd had to add collecting the guns and booty to his case work. He didn't want to know about anything else. "Don't hit any video stores for a while. Next time it'll be a cop instead of store security and an asshole with his pet gun."

"I already had something else in mind before tonight."

"What?" The question was out before he realized he didn't want to hear the answer.

Wild Bill grinned, lifting the corners of his gunfighter moustache. "Bookstores."

THREE

Macklin said, "Laurie tells me you own a bookstore."

"No, I just manage it. It's part of a chain."

Pamela Ziegenthaler looked annoyed; but since the expression seemed to be a more or less permanent fixture on her face, her son-in-law didn't think he'd offended her with his comment. Her smile, when she chose to uncase it, was worse, a pained thing with barbs that stung both ways.

She could have passed for forty, but arithmetic made her nine or ten years older, despite professional highlights in her short hair and an expert application of makeup. She looked fit in a sleeveless summer top, no jiggles under the arms and good definition in the biceps, and the resemblance between mother and daughter was such that Macklin knew his wife would keep her good looks well into middle age.

"Whatever made you choose that job?" Laurie asked. "I've never known you to get through even a magazine."

"That's an advantage, dear. You don't sell books by sitting around reading and dreaming."

Laurie, a reader, simmered in silence. Macklin felt grateful not to be the only victim of her mother's lash.

He'd gotten off on the wrong foot straight away by addressing her by her married name. She'd explained sharply that she'd resumed her maiden name after her divorce from Laurie's father, but he was sure she'd been prepared to disapprove of him before they'd met. They belonged to the same generation, for one thing, and chronologically speaking, he might have fathered Laurie himself. Also, his wife had made it clear that Pamela regarded all men with suspicion — including, presumably, the one she'd been spending time with these past several months.

"I think he's younger," Laurie had briefed him during the drive from the farmhouse. "We haven't met, but some of the things she's said gave me that impression. Don't count on it working in your favor. Mother has many good qualities, but logic isn't one of them."

So however he looked at it, Macklin was screwed. Which had removed the tension of having to work hard to give a good account of himself. She could not think less of him so long as he managed to avoid actually killing someone in her presence.

They were seated on the screened porch of Pamela's house in Myrtle, a town of about 15,000 situated just far enough away from Toledo to escape being tagged a suburb, in an upscale tract that itself comprised a kind of suburb of Myrtle. The town was an old farming village that had fallen into neglect with the decline of agriculture locally, then experienced rebirth as a place for day-trippers from Detroit and Toledo to browse the candle shops, antiques malls, and knickknack emporia that had moved in when the pharmacies and hardware stores closed. The chamber of commerce had replaced the parking meters with miniature clock towers, and a Victorian tea room served scones in the old Red Tractor Diner. Riding through town, marking the changes, Laurie had sounded like a septuagenarian revisiting the scenes of her youth.

Pamela picked up her Long Island iced tea and jingled the cubes. "I understand you're retired. Were you a dot-commer, Mr. Macklin?"

"I was in the retail camera business, strictly bricks and mortar. I sold the stores and made some good investments."

"You can't be doing too well in this economy."

Laurie smiled. "We didn't come here to borrow money, Mother. We're comfortable."

"Maybe I should borrow from you."

"I didn't know you were clipping coupons." Laurie was still smiling, but there was an edge in her voice her husband hadn't heard often. He'd given up trying to comprehend the relationship between mothers and their grown daughters.

"I might consider it, to pass the time. I get lonely here evenings. Every time Benjamin's company lays a man off, they expand his territory. I often don't see him for a week."

Benjamin was the new man in her life. Macklin asked if he was a salesman.

"He's a facilitator with a home- and building-supply firm based in Toledo. What they used to call an efficiency expert. He makes the rounds among the outlets, reviews their books and inventory, and makes suggestions on how they can improve sales without increasing costs. Or decrease costs without affecting sales. I don't pretend to understand it totally, but apparently he's quite good at what he does. When the stock market collapsed, they downsized a lot of employees who had more seniority." She sounded proud, and a little bored.

"How'd you meet, in the bookstore?" Laurie sipped her iced tea — the Midwestern variety, without alcohol. She and Macklin had agreed beforehand to stay sober.

"No, he picked me up in a bar."

Macklin got directions and went into the kitchen for napkins to clean up Laurie's spill. He came back during the explanation.

"— to see your face. It was worth it. I was sitting with friends in the lounge at Banbury Cross; that's the golf course that went in after Otto Pederson sold his hundred and sixty acres and moved to California. Henry Field, your father's old business partner, introduced us. Benjamin made up a fourth after someone dropped out. It turned out we had a lot in common. His wife left him, and he used to collect Oriental rugs. He had to sell them to pay the settlement."

"You don't collect Oriental rugs." Laurie mopped at the front of her blouse.

"I've collected salt and pepper shakers for years. It's the same thing. Anyway, we struck up a conversation, and he took me out to dinner the next night. That's been going on for six months."

"Conversation and dinner."

Pamela showed her bridgework. "Sex, too, darling. Lots of wonderful, uninhibited sex. I didn't join a convent when your father left."

Macklin asked, "Does Benjamin live in Myrtle?"

"He has a condominium in Toledo, with a view of the lake. It's beautiful. He still has one rug, in the living room. He bought it back after the settlement. It was the best in his collection, he said."

"When do we get to meet this treasure?" Laurie asked.

"Any minute now. We're his guests for dinner. Can I pour you another tea? You seem to have applied most of yours externally."

Laurie said no thanks and excused herself to use the bathroom. Alone with his mother-in-law, Macklin refilled his glass from the pitcher on the wicker table. Pamela opened a small cedar box on the table and slid a cigarette between her lips. He fished a book of matches out of a pocket and lit it.

"Thank you." She blew smoke at the screen. "I have to sneak them when Laurie's around. Sometimes I'm sorry I put her through nursing school. Do you smoke? I should have offered you one."

He shook his head, putting away the

matches. "You never know when you may have to set fire to something. I carry a pocket knife, too, but I don't whittle."

"Were you a Boy Scout?"

"I was a mechanic's son. It's the same thing."

"Like collecting Oriental rugs and salt and pepper shakers." She smiled. "Who are you, Mr. Macklin?"

"Peter. I'm the man who loves your daughter."

"No, when we're alone I'll call you Mr. Macklin. And you'll call me Mrs. Ziegenthaler. I earned that *Mrs.* and I'm keeping it. I don't believe you sold cameras for a living. You're not the salesman type. I was married to one for sixteen years."

"Would you like to see the transfer papers from when I sold the stores?"

"I'm sure they exist. I'm sure you owned stores where cameras were stocked, and may have even sold one or two. Don't try to change the subject."

He sat back and sipped his tea. Somewhere in the neighborhood a gang of kids was playing a noisy and profane game of soccer.

"I know what attracted Laurie," Pamela said. "Anyone can see you're secure financially, and you're not bad-looking, if a bit ordinary. You're a calming influence. Something's happened to her in the time you've been together, that's obvious. She's less naïve. It isn't because she's been deflowered since I saw her last. I don't kid myself that that didn't happen long before she met you. Maybe it isn't my business, but suppose it is."

He said nothing. Waiting for her to ask a question.

He didn't wait long. "We've established what Laurie saw in you. What did you see in her that brought you to my back porch?"

"Have you looked at her since her braces came off?"

"Oh, beauty. These days you can buy that over the counter, and there are women more beautiful than my daughter, with breeding and connections that would get you into any group in this country. You could do better."

"I don't agree. I'm not comfortable in groups."

She blew more smoke and flicked ash onto the terra-cotta tiles at her feet. "That's the first straight thing you've said to me. I think you're a lone old panther, and that's the way you like it. Why you should decide to take a mate so late in the game is what's got me curious. And why it should be Laurie."

A floorboard squeaked inside the house. Pamela Ziegenthaler dropped her cigarette and crushed it into a crack between tiles.

"I'll find out who you are, Mr. Macklin. It's not hard these days. These days, everyone's a private detective. Hello, dear. Peter and I have been getting to know each other. He's a mechanic's son, just like your grandfather."

Laurie had entered the porch. She sniffed the air and sat down. Her features were slightly pinched. "Papa Z's father was a diesel engineer in Stuttgart. What's this about a private detective?"

"Family skeletons. He's entitled. I told him I didn't have to hire one to find out your father was cheating on me. Laurie always was closer to my father than I was," she told Macklin. "She spent her summers on the farm, milking chickens and becoming a proper corn-fed country girl. I never took to the rural life myself. Are you seriously considering buying the old homestead? Does either of you know anything about modern farming methods?"

Laurie said, "We plan to live there, Mother, not herd cattle. There are plenty of people around who know modern farming methods who will want to lease acreage. Peter and I aren't the condo and tract-home type."

"She always was stubborn. She gets that from her father."

"Have you heard from Father?" Laurie asked.

"First of each month, regular as the calendar. The check always clears. One thing we never fought about was money. Practically the only thing. Peter knows what I'm talking about; he's divorced. There was a son, wasn't there?" She lifted her eyebrows above her glass.

"There still is," he said. "Roger. He graduated from Wayne State last year. He's backpacking through Europe."

"Such a cliché. Of course the young think they invented everything."

Laurie said, "I haven't met him yet. Peter says we'll like each other."

"Let's hope so. I imagine being a stepmother to a boy your own age has its complications."

"I'm three years older, and he won't be living with us. He has a job waiting for him when he gets back. He majored in administration and marketing."

"A salesman. Just like his father. You must be proud. Children so seldom follow in their parents' footsteps anymore."

Laurie sensed there was something behind the remark; Macklin could feel it. He was searching for a safer subject when Pamela rose, announcing that her drink needed freshening. When they were alone, Laurie asked Macklin what he and her mother had found to talk about while she was in the bathroom.

"The fact that she doesn't trust me."

"She doesn't trust anything in pants. That's why Benjamin came as such a surprise." She put down her glass. "Is she threatening to have you investigated?"

"It wasn't a threat."

"What could she find out?"

"Enough. Police records are public property."

"Can she hurt you?"

"No more than the police. Don't worry about it. I didn't marry your mother."

"I don't know how she ever talked my father into it." She put a hand on his knee. He thought she was going to kiss him, but she whispered in his ear. "I snooped in the medicine cabinet. There are some man things, a razor and a can of Barbasol. Mother uses Nair."

"Did that shock you?"

"Not after what you said. But I didn't

really believe he existed until I saw the evidence. You've seen what she's like to spend an afternoon with. Who in his right mind would practically move in with her?"

"It could be he sees something in her you don't."

She sat back. "Well, I'd just like to know more about this person."

"I take back what I said," he said. "I did marry your mother."

A door closed on the other side of the house, followed by voices. A moment later Pamela came out on the porch with a full glass in one hand and her other arm linked inside a stranger's. Macklin rose. The man was a half inch taller than he, slender in a terry sport coat with natural shoulders and olive cotton slacks, soft loafers on his narrow feet. He was close to Macklin's age, with splinters of silver in his black hair, cut in a brush that made him look older, possibly out of deference to Pamela. His features were even and unremarkable. He had a shy smile and wore no jewelry except a plain wristwatch on a leather band.

"Look what I found on the doorstep," Pamela said. "Laurie and Peter, this is Benjamin Grinnell, our host."

Macklin and Grinnell shook hands. They exerted equal pressure.

FOUR

When it was created, to handle the interstate fallout from the breakdown of order in Detroit after the 1967 race riot, the Ohio State Police Task Force on Armed Robbery was promised four floors of office space, a clerical staff of fifty, and two hundred on-duty officers. Several governors later, it continued to work out of a single story above a bank in downtown Columbus, with four full-time secretaries, a file clerk approaching the age of compulsory retirement, and a dozen temporary office workers. Thirty officers were assigned to the detail when there was no pressing need for them elsewhere. Four were in plainclothes, and one of these was Captain Edgar Prine, the task force's commander.

Somewhat surprisingly, for he never hesitated to call a press conference to complain about sloth, incompetence, or political cronyism among the top brass, Prine was never heard to complain about the force's cramped quarters and coolie status. The eleven blocks that separated him from the capitol building might as well have been eleven hundred miles, allowing him to conduct business with minimal supervision and to relax the uniform dress code, a practice he believed created *esprit de corps* unique to the officers who had actively sought the assignment. Under his tolerant eye, green neckties and pink shirts often clashed with regulation navy serge, and until Prine himself had cracked down on more blatant examples of abuse, bush hats pinned up on one side Aussie fashion and batons with notches cut in the handles had not been uncommon. The captain always wore somber tailored broadcloth and solid-color knitted ties on white or pale blue shirts, but the reporters who loitered in the bank lobby hoping to snag an interview when he came off the elevator still referred to the task force privately as Baron von Prine's Flying Circus. Unlike those bold individuals in the department who addressed him as Reverend, they never showed disrespect in his presence; Prine was always good for a colorful column when news was slow, and quick to cancel police credentials whenever he detected offense.

To the Ohioan who had not managed to

miss his frequent appearances on television, Prine's corner office was as much an icon as the man himself: the rich blue curtains, stately (and budget-bending) walnut paneling, the American and Ohio state flags on gold staffs flanking the carved mahogany desk, elevated on a dais so that when the captain rose from behind it, he overwhelmed his audience with his already intimidating height.

Few knew the room was a dummy. Prine had further incommoded his space-starved staff in order to dress a set to awe the media and important visitors such as the governor, whose own office at the capitol was larger, but not so statesmanlike as to support the presence of the larger-than-life-size bust of Lincoln on a pedestal in one corner. When the visitors had left, Prine returned to his working office next door, with its contemporary glass-topped desk and homely worktables where papers and large-scale maps could spread, while three junior men bumped knees in their shared space and damned the room that stood empty five days out of every seven. The captain had borrowed the concept from J. Edgar Hoover, a man whom to his life's regret he had never met. He was content to let others dismiss the eccentricity as another sign of megalomania, but he knew that without the show of opulence and waste, his appropriations would dry up. State legislators, like their models in Washington, distrusted austerity as some kind of pose. A hair shirt almost always concealed a private preference for silk, and thievery on the grand scale.

Prine was sitting at his real desk, up to his elbows in old arrest reports, when a fax came in with an IdentiShop likeness of the man the captain believed was the case man in the latest video-store robbery. He studied the crudely blocked-out, computer-generated features briefly, then used his intercom to summon Farrell McCormick, his assistant.

"Mac, this face trip any wires?"

McCormick, a detective lieutenant with twenty-seven years' experience in law enforcement, the first seven with the Pickaway County Sheriff's Department, held the illustration out at arm's length. A vainer man than his superior, he never wore glasses in company. When he addressed the media, he had his prepared statements printed out in eighteen-point type so he would not be seen to squint. Despite that egocentricity, he was a drab and rather dusty party in suit coats that didn't quite match his trousers, whose hair was cut at home by his wife, a woman with no talent in that area, and who had failed to qualify on the state police shooting range his last three times out. Prine falsified the results in order to keep his best detail man on duty. McCormick never forgot a face or an MO, could match the one to the other almost instantly from his photographic memory of thousands of files going back many years.

He returned the fax. "No, but God doesn't build 'em from a kit. I look at these composites and all I see is Nose B-slash-this, Chin F-slash-that. Ears from Column A. We never should've done away with police artists."

"I could dig one up, but by this time that cashier wouldn't recognize the guy if we printed his face directly from her head. We'll make copies anyway, send them out to all the posts. Not to the media. Let's hold the crackpot calls to double digits. Do you see this guy in a ski mask?"

"Maybe. Probably not, though. We sure these are the same guys that hit the other three stores? This is the first time it's come to shooting."

"Three inside, all in green shirts. The colors change, but they always dress alike. Say a fourth behind the wheel, judging by how fast they spun out. Shotgun and two handguns. Plus they always hit the same chain. That's where the money is. What do you think?"

"They're pros. When the shooting starts, they won't shoot each other, on account of the uniform. We ought to have a line on them by now." McCormick sounded petulant. That was his area.

Prine said, "Not if they never ran together before the first job. Which means they were recruited. They take the credit-card slips. Who do we know with the resources you need to put them in circulation?"

"Oh. Those guys."

"The case man's running liaison."

"Cleveland?"

"Or Toledo."

McCormick nodded. "Joe Vulpo."

"Joe's been nutty for years. So's his boy Tommy, but he isn't at the pajama stage yet. The old man won't step down, and the other old-timers don't trust Tommy enough to make it official, but someone has to call the shots. He's got a little regency going up there."

"I'd prefer Cleveland," McCormick said.

"Me, too. You never know which way a lunatic's going to jump."

"It's Toledo."

"Why should our luck change now?"

"Pull in Tommy?"

Prine drummed together the police reports on all four robberies, putting the IdentiShop sketch on top. "We'll make a social call. I'd rather talk to a nut than his lawyer."

FIVE

Peter and Laurie had booked a room in Toledo, in a resort hotel on the lake that required a nonrefundable deposit for the first night in advance. It had given them an excuse to decline Pamela Ziegenthaler's halfhearted offer to put them up. They had turned down after-dinner drinks in order to get on the road early.

The restaurant Benjamin Grinnell had taken them to, an elegant place with candles on the tables in a large ugly block building that had once been an icehouse, had served lobsters and rack of lamb on china platters carried by waiters in livery. The service was better than the food, but in Myrtle the tradition of fine dining was no older than the CLOSED notice on the last farm-equipment store.

Laurie had asked their host about his work.

"It's dull to the outsider," he said, cracking an underdone claw. "Somewhat terrifying from inside. You're always going someplace you've never been, telling strangers what they're doing wrong, and suggesting a better way than the one they've followed for years. That's one thing when you're talking to a bookkeeper, and quite another when it's the floor supervisor with a box cutter in his hand. These days there's a lot of rage in the workplace."

"Were you ever attacked?"

Her mother spoke. "Benjamin likes to dramatize. So far Arnold Schwarzenegger hasn't come calling, asking for the rights to his life story."

"You're absolutely right, Pamela. I'm just a CPA on wheels. Would anyone care for more wine?"

Laurie had wanted to stab her mother with a fork. But Benjamin had appeared relieved. Either he was uncomfortable being the center of attention or Pamela had spared him the embarrassment of being caught in a self-aggrandizing lie. In any case, the rest of the evening had been dismal. Conversation was strained, as by tacit agreement all had refrained from commenting on the food.

Peter had been driving for some minutes in silence when Laurie broke the peace.

"Was your father really a mechanic?"

"He owned a garage."

"That isn't what I asked."

"He was a loan shark. He did some heavyweight work on the side. They called them mechanics back then. It was a long time ago."

"Heavyweight work. As in killing?"

"Only if it couldn't be avoided. Killing never was good for business, no matter what you've seen on *The Sopranos.* Some roughing around, maybe a broken bone or two. He died when I was little."

"Died."

" 'Died suddenly,' the obituary said. The front page said something else. He was forty-one."

She didn't say anything for a quarter mile. Headlights were scarce in the westbound lanes. Except for late Saturday night and the four p.m. rush hour, there was always more traffic going toward Toledo than coming from it. That much hadn't changed since she was a girl.

"You never had a chance, did you?" she said.

"We all have the same chances. I could've taken auto shop."

"Are you always this hard on yourself?"

"Only lately."

She thought about that and finally fished a compliment to her out of it.

"What did you think of Benjamin?" she asked.

"Your mother seems happy with him."

"Does she? I can't tell. She's incapable of expressing an emotion. There always has to be irony."

"A psychiatrist would call that a defense mechanism."

"I call it a pain in the butt. You didn't answer my question. What did *you* think of him?"

He said nothing.

She looked at him. His profile was immobile in the lights spaced out along the interstate. "You didn't like him?"

"I didn't say that."

"I know. You didn't say anything. That's always a sure sign."

He was quiet so long she thought he'd decided not to answer.

"I think he's a player."

"A player."

"I could be wrong."

"I don't know what a player is," she said. "I'm still learning the language."

"Don't learn it too well. A player is what I am. Or what they call me when they don't use words like heavyweight and mechanic."

She laughed. "That's ridiculous."

"I could be wrong."

"He could barely crack the shell on his lobster. He's polite and boring, except for that story about a floor supervisor with a box cutter. I think Mother likes him because she can dominate him. He's the most nonthreatening man I think I've ever met."

"After me." Peter sounded amused.

"A man can be quiet without harboring guilty secrets. You don't know my mother. She'd never let a man near her if she thought he wasn't on the up-and-up. I'm surprised she ever let *any* man into her life after Father. But Benjamin's as far from my father as you could expect to find. He was a backslapper, a man's man, and when he drank too much he got loud. She would never have gone with him to a restaurant like the one we went to tonight. He'd have embarrassed her by hitting on a waitress."

"They didn't have waitresses."

"A female customer, then. She put up with it until she found out he was taking them back to his hotel when he was on the road. After that there were scenes."

"I guess that's why you picked me."

They slowed down when they entered a construction zone. A bank of blinding lights illuminated a crew pouring asphalt onto a closed lane.

"I see what you're getting at," she said,

once the lane opened. "Just for the sake of argument, what would a player be doing romancing Pamela Ziegenthaler? She likes to put people on the spot, but she's hardly the gun-moll type."

"I never heard anyone call anyone a gun moll outside a movie theater. I don't think anyone else has, either. Not since Dillinger was running around."

"Well, whatever you call them now. I just found out what a player is."

"I romanced you," he said.

"You were looking for someone to reform you. Mother doesn't have that kind of patience."

"You're probably right."

Traffic thickened as they entered the outskirts of the city, and Peter concentrated on looking for their exit. A sign came up announcing it in two miles.

"Something's on your mind besides Benjamin," Laurie said then.

"I have to go into Detroit tomorrow afternoon. I'll be back before dark. Dorfman wants a meeting."

Laurie's heartbeat quickened. Loyal Dorfman was a retired criminal attorney, the former head of a large firm that had represented athletes and other celebrities charged with felonies. It had serviced mob defendants until the RICO laws proved impossible to beat. "Has something gone wrong with the case?"

"Texas wants to extradite, for Davis and Edison. He thinks it's just a feint, to make him second-guess his strategy. But he wants to confer."

"Not California?"

"No evidence. Anyway, they were trying to indict Maggiore. I saved L.A. County a million in prosecutors' fees alone."

"*We* did. I drove the car, remember?"

"No, and neither do you."

"If I find out you're protecting me at your own risk, I'll come forward and confess."

"It won't come to that." He put on the blinker. "I think Dorfman just wants to reassure himself I won't panic and take a deal."

"Why don't you?"

"Because I'd hang myself waiting for the trial date."

"Oh." She changed the subject. "He could reassure himself over the phone. He charges seven hundred an hour for consultation."

"I don't discuss business over the phone."

"You're sure that's all it is, a feint?"

"I'll find out tomorrow."

They exited the freeway. Laurie snapped on the map light and read aloud the directions they'd been given by the hotel. When after a few blocks they determined the information was right, she switched off the light. "When were you planning to tell me about going to see Dorfman?"

"When I did. I didn't say anything before because I didn't want to spoil your time with your mother. I knew you'd worry. And I was right."

"I thought we might see the real-estate agent tomorrow."

"It's been on the market for months. It'll still be there day after tomorrow. We don't want to seem eager."

"You're sure you want to live in the country?"

"I've had it with city living. If you keep your curtains open, all the neighbors know your business, and if you keep them closed, they get too curious wondering what your business is."

"It's the same in the country. The rumor mill never closes. Anyway, we don't have any business. I may go back to work someday, but you're retired. It bothers me that I keep having to remind you of that."

"I didn't mean *business* business. I meant

the daily routine. Wherever you live, I want to live with you."

She was overcome with sudden emotion. She reached over and squeezed his thigh, and if he weren't so serious about his driving, she'd have crept her hand up farther.

In the hotel room they made love with the passion of their honeymoon. It left them soaked and panting. Later, listening to his even breathing in the dark, she was sorry she'd thought of their honeymoon. That was when she'd killed a man.

It was self-defense, and it wasn't as if she'd planned it, but it wasn't the kind of wedding-week memory she'd hoped to carry into old age. Sleepless nights had followed, small eternities of self-loathing and regret, and when she did sleep, the dreams were always waiting. In her daylight exhaustion she had considered therapy, and in the next moment abandoned the idea. Analysts took an oath of confidence, but analysts were human, and she'd lost her faith in the race. Then would come the law to separate her and Peter forever. Peter had seen her torment, but he couldn't help her with something he'd never experienced, or if he ever had, it had happened so long ago it had lost its sting. She'd faced it alone.

Time was proving itself the remedy. Time, and her increasing awareness that Peter intended to keep his promise never to return to his old life or to maintain secrets, had brought her this far, but there was still a long way to go, and if she ever reached a point where what she'd done no longer haunted her, what did that say about her worth as a person? As a wife, and as the mother she hoped someday to be? If she taught values to her children and was not repelled by her own hypocrisy, what kind of monster did that make her?

And it had not been just one man. If you counted complicity, she had killed two. The second time she had driven the car. She'd been the getaway, the wheel, and if she consoled herself that she had stayed in the car and had had no direct part in the act, she was left with the knowledge that that time it had been cold-blooded murder, an execution planned from start to finish. It had been in defense of Peter, because the man would certainly have tried to kill him another time, as he had before, by proxy, without pulling a trigger or even touching a weapon. But if she had exonerated herself on those grounds, she would have begun the short straight slide toward becoming a habitual offender. Because it had been easier the second time.

She knew then why she'd suggested buying her grandfather's old farm. By returning to a childhood place, she would erase the crimes of adulthood. But there was another explanation, more sinister. She would remove herself physically from the company of people. From her potential victims.

"Peter." She shook him.

He shuddered and was awake. She saw his eyes gleaming in the moonlight reflecting off Maumee Bay, around the edges of the blinds that covered the window.

"Did you mean what you said before about Benjamin?"

"I could be wrong." His voice was clear, as if sex and sleep had not interrupted a conversation hours old.

"How can you find out?"

SIX

In terms of the colorful, relatively young history of mob activity in the city of Toledo, Joe Vulpo was one of the founding fathers.

He was born Giuseppe Garibaldi Vulpone in 1915, aboard the *S.S. Mauritania*, bellowing his protests just inside United States territorial waters; which had proven crucially significant sixty years later, when the U.S. Department of Justice attempted to deport him to Sicily on charges stemming from labor racketeering and organized crime in interstate commerce. Declared a citizen by three minutes and two hundred yards, Vulpo was instead sentenced to a year in the federal correctional institution in Marion, Illinois, and released after ten months for good behavior.

His first experience with organized crime in interstate commerce had taken place at age eighteen, when he'd accompanied a caravan led by Pete Licavoli from Detroit to challenge the Purple Gang's monopoly of the trade in bootleg liquor and assassination-for-hire in Toledo. Like Cicero, Al Capone's lair away from home outside Chicago, the Ohio port city had been governed and policed by big-city gangsters for years, in this case Jews, but Licavoli thought it was time for new management. Vulpo had rattle-banged across the state line in the back of a beer truck with a dozen other young men armed with blackjacks, pistols, and lethal garlic breath. He never returned to Michigan.

Buried in the yellowing files of the *Toledo Blade* and the *Cleveland Plain Dealer* were the shrill headlines and accompanying grainy photos of bombed-out storefronts, bullet-riddled sedans, and splayed corpses that had marked the Sicilians' victory and subsequent assumption of all contraband traffic south of Monroe and along the lake shoreline as far east as Buffalo.

Vulpo, of course, had played no larger part in the campaign than that of common street soldier. Apart from the occasional arrest and one conviction for aggravated assault (for which he served ninety days in the Wood County Jail), he'd escaped official notice until 1957, when he was one of the men detained for questioning following the police raid on the legendary crime conference in Apalachin, New York. By 1960, his FBI file filled two drawers, including stenotyped interviews with confidential informants and transcripts of conversations recorded from wiretaps. In addition to having partnerships in casinos in Las Vegas and Havana, he was suspected of investing money from a union pension fund in a narcotics operation based in British Honduras, and alleged to be one of the nine men who sat on the commission that ran the American Mafia.

The Department of Justice attempted to indict him several times during the twelve years that followed his stretch in Marion. Three grand juries failed to hold him over for trial, and the first time he was tried, the judge called for acquittal when the government's star witness admitted that he'd agreed to testify against Vulpo in return for a *nol-pros* on an old perjury charge. It was at this time the newspapers christened Vulpo the Iron Boss, declaring him impregnable to law enforcement.

Then came the Racketeer Influenced and Corrupt Organizations Act, and the Iron Boss began to show signs of corrosion. In effect, RICO repealed the Bill of Rights without going to the states, enabling investigators to bug priests' confessionals and attorneys' offices and tap the telephones of everyone associated with the suspect. Responding to the evidence thus gathered, a jury found Vulpo guilty on eight counts of violating RICO. When his appeals ran out in 1990, however, Vulpo was in custody in the Ottawa County Jail for indecent exposure. He'd been observed walking along the Ohio Turnpike wearing nothing but a pair of hand-loomed cashmere socks, and arrested by sheriff's deputies.

Thus began a series of bizarre incidents during which the seventy-five-year-old racketeer's mental state came into question. Released into the custody of his son Thomas, he stuck his tongue into a light socket in an upstairs bedroom of Thomas's home in Northwood and was taken to the St. Vincent Medical Center for treatment. Ten days later, back in Northwood, city officers found him lying in the parking lot of a roadhouse, unconscious with three cracked ribs and bleeding from an open head wound. Upon investigating they learned that he had attracted unwelcome attention from members of the Buckeye Bastards Motorcycle Club when he urinated on the club president's chinos in the crowded men's room. Witnesses reported that finding all the urinals taken, the victim had stood back and taken aim between the president's legs, missing his target by several inches. When the officers called his son's house from St. Vincent, Thomas expressed surprise that his father was not upstairs in bed. On still another occasion, the Iron Boss was detained by private security at a Toledo Wal-Mart for masturbating in the aisle in Home Fashions.

Agents of the Justice Department were unmoved, insisting that Vulpo was trying to avoid incarceration on a mercy plea of diminished capacity. Greater gangdom disagreed. Vulpo, who had a reputation for conducting himself with dignity and a nearly obsolete sense of honor, was now known in the bars and restaurants where the cognoscenti hung out as Joey Loops. Those with bachelor's degrees called him Don Compos Mentis.

In the natural order of things, the old man's infirmities would elevate either his lieutenant or his son to his position as head of the Toledo crime family. However, his longtime sub capo, Paul Scalpini, was three years into his own fifteen-year sentence for RICO violations, and his son Thomas was regarded among the veterans who served his father as dangerously unstable. The rumor persisted that Tommy

Vulpo had attended his graduation ceremonies at OSU wearing high-heeled pumps under his robes, and he had been questioned by the police on several occasions when transvestite prostitutes complained that they'd been picked up, brutally beaten, sodomized, and dumped into gutters from a car whose description matched Tommy Vulpo's custom-built Bentley. There weren't many Bentleys wandering the streets of Toledo, and fewer still with redwood bars built into the backseats. Although none of the victims got a good look at their assailant, most recalled the squat neck and shaved head of the man in the driver's seat. Yet they failed to pick Take, the younger Vulpo's Romanian bodyguard and chauffeur, out of lineups, and in time all the complaints were withdrawn.

As a result, Thomas Anthony Vulpo had a clean sheet with the law. This was not the case with his father's loyal followers, whose faith in modern police methods was higher than that of the average solid citizen. Crazy Joe's eccentricities were considered harmless, but Terrible Tommy's reflected seriously antisocial behavior of the sort that interfered with the smooth operation of a family concern with a tradition as old as AT&T's. In addition, Tommy was given to unpredictable rages, and had been known to strike the faithful Take in the presence of witnesses. They refused to meet with the son unless the father was present, and whenever Tommy issued an instruction, their eyes went to Joe to see if he nodded. The old man always seemed alert during meetings, even if he did sometimes attend them wearing a Porky Pig baseball cap and a T-shirt reading '69 OLYMPIC MUFF-DIVING TEAM.

By the time Ben Grinnell was summoned to meet with Tommy Vulpo following the violent outcome of the latest video-store robbery, Joe was eighty-seven, in failing health, and his presence during meetings was erratic. Many of the old guard were gone — dead, ill, or imprisoned — and the younger lieutenants, some of whom barely remembered a time when the Iron Boss was in full command of his faculties, didn't insist upon the old man's presence, tacitly accepting Tommy's authority. A rift had opened between the generations, with the able-bodied seniors running their franchises more or less independently of Northwood — albeit continuing to make their contributions to the executive fund — while the younger men carried out instructions from Tommy. This feudal situation had weakened the organization's structure, giving federal and local officers an opportunity to insert a wedge between the factions, isolate the more vulnerable elements, and prosecute them for legions of petty crimes that would ordinarily have been defended vigorously by attorneys on retainer to the Vulpo family. The implication was clear: Support Tommy Vulpo or battle the barracuda on your own.

The loss of manpower to various penal institutions, and of the revenue it had supplied, forced Northwood to follow the lead of legitimate corporations in a bad economy and downsize. Heavyweight work once conducted by "made" men in good standing with the family was farmed out to independents — non-Sicilians mostly, including Puerto Ricans and blacks — expense accounts were slashed, and single-area specialists obliged to assume responsibilities not covered in their original job descriptions.

Naturally, there had been protests, most vocally from among those factions that had all but seceded from Northwood. But they'd ceased after the disappearance of James "Jimmy Teats" D'Onofrio during his journey home from his niece's wedding in

Louisville, Kentucky, and the discovery six weeks later of the badly decomposed remains of Vincent Manila in the spacious trunk of his beloved Oldsmobile 98, recovered from the bottom of a flooded quarry in rural Pennsylvania. Both men had been associated with Joe Vulpo since the early days of the World War II black market, and they had joined in demanding the resignation — peacefully, if necessary — of Tommy after the effects of the budget crunch hit home. Not since the last great gang war in 1972 had anyone of such high rank made the final sacrifice; two seemed just short of excessive. Even the federal drones who spent their days hunched over tape recorders eavesdropping on the dreary Vulpo domestic routine were impressed.

A sea change occurred on September 11, 2001. Gangsters seemed warm and fuzzy compared to foreign terrorists at the controls of passenger jets. Law enforcement directed its attention away from the American underworld and toward national security. Quietly, the dysfunctional Ohio crime family hailed this gift from the Middle East. Arrests fell off, and peace reigned. Joe Vulpo celebrated by climbing down a trellis and skinny-dipping in Swan Creek Park.

★ ★ ★

Grinnell swung his Lexus into the composition doughnut driveway and parked in front of Tommy Vulpo's house, a crazy-quilt collage of architectural styles from English Tudor to Walter Gropius, and testament to its owner's tendency toward multiple personalities. Take was waiting for him on the top steps when he got out of the car, not a good sign. Grinnell had underestimated the homebound traffic into the suburbs and was fifteen minutes late for his appointment. Depending upon the state of Tommy's chemistry that day, the lapse would either pass unmentioned or trigger a tantrum, complete with flying spittle and possibly a heavy desk accessory. You never knew with him, that was the unsettling thing. He was calmer when his father was present, but in recent months the old man had been absent frequently, with only the sound of his heavy footfalls patrolling the floor above to indicate he was at home. Rumor said he was expecting Mussolini to invade by way of Lake Erie.

Take was a Romanian national. He had no hair on his head, not even in his nose, and the flattened skull characteristic of his race, falling in a plane to the back of his collar. He wore a brown leather windbreaker indoors and out, concealing an underarm holster, fawn-colored corduroys, and bare feet, the same uniform he wore when he drove Tommy in the Bentley. The extent of his understanding of English was unknown. Tommy had recruited him from a line waiting to register as aliens. He was thought to have been among the refugees who fled eastern Europe after the USSR fell, and that the shoes he'd worn in Lubyanka Prison had ruined his feet for shoes of any kind. The story on the pavement was he'd smuggled himself past Immigration to avoid prosecution for crimes against humanity as a member of Nikolai Ceausescu's secret police. Grinnell was almost certain the story had been circulated by Tommy Vulpo to intimidate potential attackers. The bodyguard inspected Grinnell for weapons and escorted him to Tommy's study on the ground floor.

The house was three stories high, with each floor converted to a self-contained apartment complete with kitchen, bedrooms, and entertainment facilities, and each with its own entrance and separate staircase to the connecting floors. The ground floor was Tommy's, the second his estranged wife Sylvia's, and the top belonged to Joe after his move from the original family home in Toledo. Tommy had had the stove in his father's apartment disconnected and ornamental but functional bars installed in the windows to prevent accidents and escapes. It was just about the most dismal household arrangement Grinnell had ever heard of.

Bright carpeting, as green as a golf course, covered the floor of the study, which was decorated in Danish Modern. The bookshelves, desk, and occasional tables were bleached a light blonde against the six-month Scandinavian night and similarly bleak Ohio winter. Tommy Vulpo took his attention from the pornographic Web site on the computer monitor on his desk to greet Grinnell and offer refreshment. The visitor declined. Take was dismissed. The site, Grinnell observed, was devoted to photographs of obvious males in lace lingerie and spike heels.

Tommy was a youthful-looking forty-five. His face had been lifted, his hair highlighted and curled into Grecian ringlets, and in the white terry-cloth robe he always wore as a dressing gown he bore a strong resemblance to the Roman emperor with an unfortunate speech impediment in *Monty Python's Life of Brian*. He had fine features, which for once were arranged in a smile. He invited Grinnell to sit.

One refreshing thing — the only — about Tommy was his tendency not to engage in small talk. "What happened in Hilliard?"

Hilliard was the Columbus suburb where the most recent video-store robbery had taken place. When Grinnell hesitated, Tommy told him the room had been swept that morning for electronic surveillance.

"The manager came running out of the back room with a gun. The shotgun man had no choice but to open fire."

"Did you see the manager before the shooting?"

"I saw him. I thought he was a customer. I was sure he wasn't an undercover officer." Grinnell was in the habit of never volunteering fault or denying it. Both attitudes left a man open to assault in the circles he'd moved in since age fourteen.

"You're an experienced case man. How'd that happen?"

"It shouldn't happen, but it does. It's almost impossible to predict when a hometown hero will turn up."

"It's rotten business. No one cares except the cops when a multimillion-dollar chain gets ripped off. Shooting citizens brings down heat. Even when the citizen's an asshole."

"I advised the leader of the crew to back off for a while."

"Was he amenable?" Tommy was looking at the Web site.

"He agreed to shift targets. Bookstores."

"Any money there?"

"I didn't think so, until I researched it. A chain store in a good location can take in as much as ten thousand on Friday night."

"Cash?"

"And credit cards. That's our end."

"I know what's our fucking end! I spent two rotten summers as a teenager helping strike off duplicate cards from filthy carbons. Don't tell me what's our fucking end!"

Grinnell managed not to jump when Tommy started screaming. He'd known there was seldom any buildup. He said nothing.

Tommy wiped his mouth with the heel of a hand. Grinnell had never actually seen him frothing, but Tommy believed his own legend as well as anyone. When he spoke again his voice was level.

"When an employee fucks up, it's normal to relieve him of his responsibilities. I think they learn more by taking on additional ones. From now on, you're in charge of buying and delivering weapons.

It's risky, and a pain in the ass, but not that much more than disposing of them, which you've been doing for a while. Maybe you'll keep your eyes open next time."

Grinnell was afraid his punishment would take such a form. But as he'd been more afraid that it would take another, he made no complaint. "Where do I buy them?"

"Do I look like I'd know that? Show some initiative, for chrissake." Tommy clicked his mouse. The next page that came up looked like a Broadway tribute to fellatio. It was a dismissal.

Outside the study, Grinnell nearly collided with the Iron Boss.

Joe Vulpo was dressed respectably enough, although sloppily, in a wrinkled sport shirt that might have doubled as a pajama top, with half the tail hanging out over the trousers of an old gray pinstripe suit, baggy in the knees, and carpet slippers worn nearly through at the toes. There was white in his stubble and his thinning gray hair stuck up comically on one side. His face looked bloated and his eyes lacked focus.

"My sheets are all wet," he told Grinnell. "Change them right away."

Before Grinnell could explain he wasn't the housemaid, Take materialized and took the old man's arm gently, but in a grip that would snap bone if resisted. "What you doing down here, Don Vulpo? How you get out?"

With a shy smile, Joe held out his free hand. On the palm lay a bent nail and what looked like the plastic refill from a ballpoint pen. Grinnell suspected that he'd spent part of his early life as a picklock. Take scooped the contraband out of the old man's hand and conducted him toward the stairs.

"What about my sheets?"

"You don't pee on them if you wear your diapers."

Grinnell got into his car and started down the driveway. Near the end he made room for a wide-bodied sedan on its way up. It was a plain car of indeterminate American make, rounded just enough at the corners to satisfy modern aerodynamics, yet still reminiscent of the slab-sided barges of the 1970s. It was demonstrably an official vehicle.

The face behind the wheel was vaguely familiar. He thought he might have seen it on television or in the newspapers, always off from center. But the man seated beside the driver jolted his memory like an electrode. Wide-bodied like the car, his height crowding the headliner, he was as much a fixture of Ohio culture as Chief Wahoo. Most recently, Grinnell had seen him reading a statement on TV and answering questions from reporters in connection with the Hilliard robbery. It was no great leap from there to the reason State Police Captain Edgar Prine was coming to see Tommy Vulpo.

SEVEN

"A lot of changes since you were in town last," Loyal Dorfman said. "Casinos. Mexicantown. They knocked down Hudson's finally, and elected a new mayor. I say *they*. I haven't voted since Truman. That mean little cocksucker put me off politics for good."

Macklin said nothing, waiting for the old lawyer to wind down. They were seated at the round oak table in the bay window of his dining room in Redford Township, fifteen minutes from downtown Detroit. The house had been built in 1944, and he had claimed it from the original owner when the owner couldn't pay his fee for legal services. Most of Dorfman's old law office — desk, files, barrister cases, seventy volumes of federal and state precedents — was in storage in the attic. Since his retirement from daily practice, he preferred to work in his dining room with the aid of a laptop. Most of his current clients were professional criminals who drew confidence from the lack of a visible system of records. He was a patrician-looking eighty, with a polar cap of white hair brushed immaculately and a long, blue-veined nose suitable for looking down at witnesses for whose testimony he held small regard. Even in his leisure he continued to wear three-piece woolen suits with matching necktie and display handkerchief sets. He'd been disbarred once, and won a headline-making suit to reinstate his license. The front page of the old *Detroit Times* announcing his victory hung in a frame next to his 1948 diploma from the University of Michigan School of Law and a dozen birthday cards signed by his great-grandchildren.

From the kitchen at the other end of the house came the clatter of pots and pans and crockery, the homely clangor of Mrs. Dorfman's daily assault on dirty dishes. She was as deaf as a fence rail and no threat to the sanctity of the attorney-client relationship. Macklin enjoyed the comfort of the informal setup; it was far more difficult for the FBI to bug a private home whose occupants seldom left, and never both at the same time.

"What's Texas up to?" he asked, when Dorfman finally ran out of small talk.

"The usual bullshit. They say they've got

an eyewitness who can place you at Davis's home the night he was killed."

"Who?"

The lawyer pecked with one finger at a series of keys on the laptop, frowned at the screen. "Neighbor named George Hogstroop. He picked you out of a mug file as the man he saw speeding away after someone shot out the rear window of his parked Corvette."

Macklin remembered the incident in detail. He'd used a slingshot to fire a steel ball bearing through the window. The owner had come charging out of his house with a shotgun, drawing a trio of officers out of a surveillance van and allowing Macklin to enter Davis's house unnoticed. But Macklin hadn't sped away after committing the act of vandalism. He'd let himself out of his parked rental car while the officers were arresting the Corvette owner and finished the job on foot.

"He didn't see anything," Macklin said. "They bullied him into making the identification after they found out I was in town that day. They had a laundry list of disturbing-the-peace violations against him. If you check into it, you'll find the charges were dropped."

"I did. They were. I thought it was

something like that. I know some people in San Antonio. He'll recant."

"What about Edison?"

Edison — Macklin knew him by no other name — had been the spotter on the Davis job. He'd made the mistake of letting Macklin know he knew his name. Macklin had mopped that one up on his way out of town.

"Nothing there. San Antonio knew he had ties to Old Man Rivera, and he was shot in the face with a single slug from a thirty-eight revolver, so they thought of you. You ought to consider a new choice in weapons."

"I'm retired."

"Me, too." Dorfman bared his false teeth in a shark's smile. It made him look less aristocratic. "I just wanted to make sure we covered everything the last time we spoke. Men in your walk of life have a habit of squirreling things away, even from those best in a position to help them."

"I told you everything." Everything about San Antonio. Since Los Angeles had closed the investigation into the murder later in the week of Carlo Maggiore, he'd seen no reason to provide information the lawyer didn't need to pursue his case against the People of the State of Texas.

Also, there was the sticky point that Laurie had been indirectly involved in the L.A. matter.

Dorfman's predatory grin remained in place. "Okay, we're done."

"That's it?"

"I'll be in touch if anything comes up. I think we can drag this out until Austin loses interest. Johns Davis and Richard Edison were known members of the underworld. No one's likely to lose an election over either of them, and anyway the situation's changed in this country. You can thank your lucky stars you're not an Arab. I've been asked to defend some suspected terrorists."

"Just asked?"

"And answered. I have standards."

Macklin looked at the clock on the sideboard. Seven hundred dollars gone in five minutes. He was determined to use up more of his hour.

"Do you know any people in Toledo?" he asked.

"My granddaughter lives there with her husband and two children."

Dorfman's Rolodex — if he'd ever become insane and kept one — had more unlisted numbers belonging to the *Fortune* 500 list of notorious felons than any in

Washington. Three subpoenas, including one served by the U.S. Attorney General in person, had failed to make him surrender them or even admit he knew their owners. He'd celebrated his seventy-fifth birthday in federal custody for contempt of Congress, and been rewarded for his continued silence with an annual IRS audit. But his smile dissolved before the blank wall of Macklin's face.

"I know some people," the lawyer said then. "This have anything to do with your case?"

"It's a personal favor. I'm looking for information on a man who calls himself Benjamin Grinnell. He says he works for a home- and building-supply business with headquarters in Toledo."

Dorfman mouthed the name silently, entering it into his personal memory bank. He kept his hands away from the computer.

"I'm still an officer of the court. If I gave you information on this Grinnell and someone gaffed him out of the Maumee River a week later, you'd be in the market for another attorney."

"He's dating my mother-in-law. The favor's for my wife."

"And how is your child bride?"

"She's fine. How are your daughter and her two children in Toledo?"

They regarded each other across the table.

The lawyer pulled at his nose, as if it weren't long enough for all the places he had to stick it into. "I've never heard of anyone named Grinnell."

"How long before you do?"

"How long before you check out of your hotel?"

Macklin drove eight miles out of his way to cruise past his old house in Southfield. He wasn't sure why. It had been a wedding present from his first employer, Mike Boniface, and he'd moved in with his first wife right after their honeymoon. It had been the first home he'd called his own. Most of the firsts of his life had taken place there, yet he had few good memories of his time within its walls. He'd raised a son there, worried about his grades and his companions, had loved there and fallen out of love. He didn't miss the coldness that had crept in like black mold and that had come away with him when he'd moved out. That had lifted only when he'd met Laurie.

The postwar two-story frame had acquired new windows — the aluminum-framed kind that resisted drafts and fresh air in equal measure — and a coat of buttery yellow paint. The color was a distinct aesthetic improvement over the layers of conventional white stretching back to Eisenhower. A basketball hoop had sprouted above the garage door; he'd meant to get around to installing one for years and felt resentment toward the homeowner who had succeeded where he'd failed. He wondered what the current occupants thought of the soundproofed basement.

There was a bicycle on the small front lawn, and in the driveway a Big Wheel tricycle (two children). A riot of blossoms burst out of boxes under the windows facing the street (a wife, probably; male flower fanciers tended toward more difficult and time-consuming projects like roses and dahlias). A Ford Expedition, that year's model, stood in the driveway. He postulated a second car in the garage. Two breadwinners under one roof. He accelerated discreetly and didn't look back.

It didn't occur to him until later that he'd evaluated everything as if he were collecting intelligence on a potential target. He wondered if he'd ever be Joe Average, with nothing on his mind but next month's mortgage payment and the dead spot in the backyard.

EIGHT

Laurie had done a lot of growing up in a short amount of time; enough growing up to decide there were two things about her character she disliked intensely, but too short an amount of time to know what to do about them.

Thing No. 1: She could feel sorry for herself at the drop of a hat. Thing No. 2: When she felt sorry for herself, she spent money.

When she took a cab from the hotel to North Towne Square, she knew she was getting back at Peter for deserting her on almost no notice at all. That understanding gave her hope for her salvation, along with the irritating knowledge that she could do nothing about it other than see it through.

Then, in a narrow deep shop crowded with clothing carousels and the aggressive personality of the owner, a gargoyle of a woman in a muumuu with overdrawn black eyebrows and huge, patently window-glass spectacles, she found that Holy Grail of female fashion, the Little Black Dress.

It was her size, scooped front and back, and sleeveless. The price was high enough to give pause, but not so high that a less patient husband than Peter would turn her out on the street, either to return it or to find her own source of income to pay for it. When she tried it on, her reflection in the dressing-room mirror drove every negative thought out of her head. The neckline was daring but not scandalous; she knew just which earrings she would wear with it, to call attention to her neck — her best feature — and away from what her mother used to call her "naughty bits"; but not so far away that strangers might not have a reason to admire them. She liked the way the color showed off her tan and the toning of her upper arms, her reward for working out regularly. When a young woman married an older man, it was important not to let oneself go.

She stepped out, walked around, and managed a clandestine twirl before the shop owner descended, chirping compliments. There was just enough rayon to make the dress move easily, with the flirty flip she sought, but enough weight so that it draped elegantly when she walked and stood still. Reluctantly she changed back into her street clothes.

The lady gargoyle was ringing up the purchase when Laurie realized a fundamental flaw in the transaction.

"I'm sorry," she said. "Could you hold it for me until later?"

The woman hoisted her black-black eyebrows above the ludicrous glasses. Her gaze flicked toward the wedding-set on Laurie's hand. "You have nothing to worry about, honey. When he sees you in it, all doubts will vanish."

Laurie felt herself flush. Did the old bat think she was a bimbo? She made her voice cool. "I'm not worried about the expense. I don't have anything to wear it to."

"If you buy it, it will come. The cosmic forces are always at work." The woman tapped a set of jeweled nails on the cash register drawer. "I close at five. If I don't hear from you by then, I'll have to put it back on the rack."

Laurie took a business card from the little Lucite rack on the counter and put it in her purse. The woman's superior attitude was so much like her mother's she decided to hold her tongue and keep the peace. Otherwise she'd have told her where else she could put the dress.

* * *

She had a salad and a Diet Sprite in the courtyard of a restaurant on the square and took a cab back to the hotel. The light was blinking on the telephone. She hoped it was Peter, but the message was from her mother, leaving the number of the bookstore and asking her to call back.

A call from Mother was always cause for anxiety, but this time it carried with it a twinge of fear. Laurie couldn't get out of her head what Peter had said about Benjamin — *I think he's a player* — and she knew at firsthand all that entailed. Was this the cry for rescue?

She spoke to an airheaded clerk, established that the "Mrs. Ziegenthaler" she'd asked for was Pamela, the clerk's boss, and caught her mother in a mood of breathless excitement, a rare event.

"I got Francis Spain!" Pamela said without greeting.

Laurie heard an insipid instrumental version of "My Heart Will Go On" playing over the store's PA system. "Who's she?"

"She's a he, my cave-dwelling child. I thought you liked to read. His first novel was only on *The New York Times* list for thirty-six weeks. *Love Song*?"

"Oh, yes." She remembered reading a review somewhere. Something about hating to kill another tree to warn readers away from a book that had leveled innocent forests. "Is that all you called about?" She was relieved; and mildly irritated. Pamela had a gift for raising Laurie's apprehensions even when she wasn't aware of them.

"*All?* You don't appreciate your mother's ingenuity. His publisher has him on a sixteen-city tour to promote the new one, *Serpent in Eden*. He was scheduled to sign at the Little Professor in Toledo, but he had some kind of fight with the chain over the way his book's being displayed. His publicist canceled. As soon as I heard, I got on the phone to our regional manager. He agreed this is our chance to cut in on the competition. He spoke to the publicist. We've got Spain for the twentieth. You must come, and bring Peter."

Laurie looked at the dates on the *TV Guide* on the nightstand. "That's next Saturday."

"Don't I know it. I've placed quarter-page ads in the *Blade* and took out a page in the *Millennium*."

"What's the *Millennium*?"

"That's right, you remember it as the *Grange*. It's the weekly rag here in town. Advertising's only one of a million things I have to do before next Saturday. I have to find a caterer and party decorations and a banner to hang outside the store. I don't know what the others are doing, but *I'm* going to have hors d'oeuvres and sparkling wine — no, champagne. No crummy cookies and cider getting stale on a paper tablecloth. I may need to apply for a permit from the village, just in case someone gets run over in the street waiting at the end of the line."

"You think that many people will show up?"

"I guess you've never been to an autograph party for an A-list author. When John Grisham signs, they hire a masseuse to prevent writer's cramp. Hell, I forgot about the masseuse. There's an Asian place on the end of town, but it looks sinister. I doubt it would be appropriate to hire one from there."

"I suppose it depends on the author. I don't know, Mother. Peter doesn't like crowds."

"Oh, that's just the signing. I'm talking about the reception *before* the signing. Just a couple of dozen people, including the president of the village council and some society. It's a chance for you and Peter to make valuable connections."

"What for? Peter's retired and I'm a nurse. Would I get to lance a better class of boil?"

"Fine. Don't come. I just thought it would be nice to have my family present at an affair that means a lot to me. Good-bye, dear."

"Wait, Mother. I'm sorry. If you'd put it that way at the start, I wouldn't have given you such a hard time. Of course we'll be there."

"No, don't put yourself out. It promises to be boring. Writers are dull company when they're not talking about their writing, and when they are, there's no shutting them up."

Laurie made a fist so tight her nails cut into her palm. She wondered if she'd ever be immune to her mother's manipulation. She forced a smile into her voice. "Well, you know me; any chance to dress up. What should I wear?"

"Do you have a cocktail dress?"

Macklin let himself into the hotel room at dusk. Laurie ran at him, threw her arms around his neck, and kissed him as if they'd been separated for a week. His muscles tensed; he'd warned her about surprising him, but his reflexes had slowed since L.A. and he didn't chop her in the throat. She smelled fresh. He was aware that he didn't, and that his beard was scratching her. "Did you leave any hot water?"

"It's a hotel, silly. They never run out."

"Obviously you've never stayed in a hotel in Mexico."

"What happened with Dorfman?"

"I didn't come back to pack my toothbrush. Can it wait till I've had a shower?"

"Should I order room service? A cake with a file in it?"

"Are you hungry?"

"I had dinner downstairs a little while ago. I meant you."

"I just want to scrub up and make love to my wife."

"So this is a conjugal visit?"

He leaned away from her. "You're going to keep doing this until I tell you everything, aren't you?"

"Uh-huh."

He told her what Dorfman had said. She studied his face, looking for cracks in his account.

"Does he really think Texas is going to give up that easily?"

"Apparently there's a bright side to foreign terrorism."

She shuddered. "What about the other thing?"

"Dorfman's making some calls. If I don't hear from him before checkout, I'll call him."

"You said you never discussed business over the phone."

"I'll just ask if he has anything for me. It might mean another quick trip to Detroit. I'm not sure what form it'll take. He's a tough old hide."

"So are you. Take your shower."

He was shaving under the warm spray when the bathroom door opened. He unscrewed his razor and removed the blade, but the shower curtain was transparent and he saw it was Laurie. He put the blade back and laid the razor in the soap receptacle. She pulled aside the curtain and stepped into his embrace. She was naked.

In bed, she fell asleep with her head on his chest. He closed his eyes, but he didn't join her. He kept seeing the house in Southfield, not as it was, but as it had been when he'd lived there, test-firing revolvers in the basement or studying surveillance reports behind the locked door of his study while Roger watched television and Donna nursed her fourth boilermaker of the evening in the living room. It had been a mistake to drive past the old place.

He decided he was less concerned with his legal case than he was with the Grinnell matter. It had been a long time since he'd had to act on anyone's behalf but his own, and now his mother-in-law had entered the circle. Then there was the possibility Grinnell knew who and what he was and had been put in place to stalk him. Macklin hoped to close out that case fast.

He looked forward to buying and moving into the farmhouse. He couldn't see himself wearing overalls or piloting a tractor; that picture was as ridiculous as a farmer holding a Glock. But nothing about the house or the acreage belonged to the world he'd known. Since their honeymoon, Macklin and Laurie had been staying in hotels and rented houses, living like vagabonds. He yearned for a foundation, if only to prevent himself from drifting back the way he'd come. He wouldn't know how to begin to give directions to there from a place like Myrtle.

Laurie was having a disturbing dream. The woman who owned the shop in North Towne Square was a real gargoyle, her jewel-clawed toes curled over the edge of a cornice. The mouth opened beneath the oversize eyeglasses and rusty water spilled out, inexplicably along with her mother's voice: *I knew you'd be back for it, honey. If you buy it, it will come.*

The image jiggled and broke up. She woke. Peter had stirred, almost dislodging her head from his chest. He was holding the paperback novel she'd left on the nightstand, staring at the garish cover. The title, *Love Song*, skirled against the wavy lines of a musical score. Francis Spain's name was as large as the title and blocked in boldly above it.

She smiled sleepily. "I see you've found out my guilty secret. I love crap."

"That doesn't say much for me." He turned to the first page. After a moment he raised an eyebrow at her.

"It gets worse," she said. "He dangles participles, splits infinitives, and uses phrases like 'off of' and 'different than.' There's a lulu on page eighteen. You'll know it when you see it."

He flipped to that page, read. He paused, then read aloud. " 'Unable to breast-feed the baby herself, Fred had to hire a wet nurse.' That almost makes sense."

"Not the kind he intended, I'm sure. I've read four chapters and there's at least one of those every couple of pages. On the plus side, he's managed to corral more clichés in the first twenty-five pages than most writers do their whole careers."

"I thought writers had editors."

"That's the scary part. What do you suppose this book was like before editing?" She kissed his chest, patted it, and laid her cheek back down. "I haven't mentioned the plot, which is even cornier than the language. I can tell you right now the heroine dies, of some beautiful poetic wasting disease, and the hero is left alone to remember her into bittersweet old age."

He read the last page. "You peeked."

"Didn't have to. Emily Brontë did it worlds better, and she died at thirty. That didn't stop a thousand others from cranking out the same story for the next hundred and fifty years. You'd think Erich Segal had emptied the well, but no."

He looked again at the cover. "Says there are over eight million copies in print. What's Spain's secret?"

"That's just the paperback. The hardcover sold another million." She sat up, pulling the sheet over her breasts, and took the book from him. She found the author's biography on the back cover. " 'Francis Spain formerly worked for a restaurant-supply dealership in Hartford, Connecticut. This is his first book.' *That's* his secret."

"What's selling restaurant supplies got to do with writing?"

"Exactly. What restaurant-supply salesman wouldn't give up his pension to become a best-selling author? It's a Cinderella story. Also he's cute." She showed him the boyish face in the picture next to the biography. Spain was a weak-chinned version of Tom Cruise.

"You call that cute?"

"Relax. Your face has character."

"No, it doesn't. If it did, I'd be dead."

"Well, I'd remember it." She waggled the book. "This is what they call a package: pretty face, heartwarming backstory. My father was a publisher's sales rep for a while. The business was beginning to look like Hollywood even then. The book itself is the smallest part of the package. Two or three patient editors can turn any frog into a prince. Or enough of one anyway not to interfere with the marketing. There's a whole section in the hotel gift shop set aside for copies of just this book. That's where I bought it."

"Why?"

"Because I wanted to know a little about

the author before we meet him." She told him about the reception.

"I guess we're going," he said after a short silence.

"Mother guilt-tripped me into it. By the way, don't tell her I bought this downstairs. She'd never forgive me for patronizing the competition."

"You're right."

"Please don't be glum. Who knows? We may have a good time. And it gave me an excuse to make a purchase."

He took back the book and looked at the spine. "Five ninety-nine. I remember when they were twenty-five cents."

"Now you sound like someone's grandfather. I didn't mean the book. Wait here."

She hopped out of bed naked, unhooked the plastic bag and hanger from the closet, and took it into the bathroom. She brushed her hair, put on light makeup, slipped the dress on over her head, made the necessary adjustments, and went back into the bedroom.

Peter was still sitting up in bed, reading *Love Song*. "You know, once you get past the fact it's crap, this isn't half —" He looked up.

She rose on the balls of her bare feet and twirled. "Do you think this will draw attention away from the guest of honor?"

"You don't need the dress for that." But she could tell by his tone he was awe-struck.

"I don't have shoes for it." She looked down at her painted toes. "Do you think we can go shopping in the morning before we leave town? I doubt I'll find what I need in Myrtle."

"My aunt had a black dress. I never saw her in it until her funeral."

"That was just a black dress. This is a little black dress. There's a difference."

"How much difference?"

She told him. She was watching herself in the full-length mirror on the closet door, turning this way and that to make the skirt flip.

"Take it off." He sounded hoarse.

She looked at him, startled. Then she looked down at the sheet covering his lap. She grinned and took off the dress.

NINE

Wild Bill sat on the back deck of his family home near Drip Rock, Kentucky, contemplating the unearthly deep green of the Daniel Boone National Forest and spinning his great-uncle Jakey's imitation Colt forward and backward on his trigger finger.

He'd seen Uncle Jakey only once, when Wild Bill's mother had hauled him by hand into a bright room where a rubber bellows wheezed and pumped air into the old man's lungs, blackened like the tin ceilings of the saloons where he'd spent his life. Jakob Berman had broken with the family in 1890, gone west in pursuit of adventure and fortune, found the first, and as to the last settled for the fake Colt, which according to family legend he'd either won playing poker or stolen off the legitimate winner after going bust. He'd spent the final six years of his very long life in a VA hospital in Lexington, his reward for service in the Spanish-American War.

The .44 revolver's counterfeit status was

confirmed by the missing *T* in the marking on the barrel, which identified it as a COL'S. It had likely been manufactured in Spain and entered the United States through Mexico sometime during the 1870s. Surface oxidation had browned the metal and turned the bone handle a tobacco-stain yellow. It was Wild Bill's only legacy, not counting the house and lot, whose back taxes he was still paying, and he'd had to commit theft in order to claim the gun.

No evidence existed to indicate that Jake Berman had been some kind of desperado, but there was enough suspicion about how he'd made his way in the West to shame Wild Bill's father, the pastor of a Lutheran church in Berea, Kentucky. The Colt knockoff had been left to Wild Bill as Jakey's youngest blood relative in a letter of intent. Samuel Berman had locked it away, not because of any danger represented by a weapon whose firing pin had rusted off, but as a protest against the outlaw taint Jakey had brought to the family. For that reason, he'd refused to allow his son to have any contact with his great-uncle when he first fell ill. Only in the shadow of death did he relent and give grudging permission to his wife to take his son for a farewell visit. He himself had stayed home, drafting a sermon on the Eighth Commandment, with veiled references to certain flaws in the parable of the Prodigal Son. Jakey had died within hours of the visit, without having regained consciousness throughout. His great-nephew had never heard his voice.

Wild Bill might have respected his father's principles if he'd simply thrown away the gun, but the thought that it had some antique value had prevented that. That strain of personal gain, so deeply seated in the descendants of pragmatic Bavarian immigrants, seemed to justify Jakey's actions while casting Samuel's into doubt. In fact, it occurred to Wild Bill that there was more honesty in robbing a bank or a train, openly and in broad daylight, than in squirreling away a wicked gift against the value it might bring with no risk involved. When Wild Bill ran away from home at age sixteen, the revolver went with him.

He'd worked his way west, washing dishes, painting houses, and burglarizing vacation homes closed for the season for anything that might be sold for quick cash. Nothing could persuade him to part with the gun. He had a childhood fascination with Western movies and the novels of

Luke Short and Louis L'Amour, and it pleased him to think he was following in Uncle Jakey's footsteps, shrugging off the chains of civilization for the freedom of the frontier. He'd hunted elk in Wyoming, worked two seasons as a fishing guide in Montana, and spent a delirious six weeks in gunfighter costume, reenacting the gunfight at the O.K. Corral for the entertainment of tourists in Tombstone, Arizona. He might have been contented to make that sort of thing a career if he hadn't received a letter from his mother's lawyer, announcing her death and calling him back to reclaim the family home in Drip Rock, along with all its debts outstanding. His father had died six years earlier of a brain aneurysm suffered while officiating at a parishioner's graveside service. The Rapture had blown out a vein.

In between legitimate occupations, Wild Bill had served a year in the Montana State Penitentiary for the armed robbery of a convenience store in Livingston and tried his hand at sticking up a train in Idaho; an enterprise abandoned when sheriff's deputies arrested him in the act of cutting down a telephone pole for the purpose of blocking the tracks. He was convicted of vandalism, served ninety days in the Madison County Jail, and upon his release was returned to Montana for six months for violation of parole. He often wondered if Uncle Jakey had encountered similar difficulties riding the outlaw trail.

His setbacks had convinced him that the law-enforcement community west of the Divide was too efficient, and too well-versed in the bandit tradition, to make that line of work profitable. Still, he loved the West, and longed to return, with a stake that would support him without running afoul of the local constabulary. Ironically, he'd been far more successful in Ohio. Video stores were easier to rob than 7-Elevens, with their gun-toting foreigners behind the counters, and the take was far better. He anticipated the same from bookstores. When the climate got too hot, as it had after that cold fish Grinnell had overlooked the renegade manager in the dirty-movie section, he had the house in Drip Rock to run to for cover.

You couldn't live in the past. He'd learned that the hard way. Things weren't the same in the twenty-first century as they had been in the nineteenth, and less so in the Midwest than in the golden West. An independent needed protection.

The organized tradition was not so well

established in Kentucky, and so he'd gone north. He'd made connections in prison that got him an introduction in Cleveland, only to find the aging organization there in a paralyzed state, rocked by a string of successful prosecutions on the federal level and disinclined to form partnerships with unpredictable outsiders. He'd been unable to secure a referral to anyone higher than the local loan sharks. Toledo was friendlier, and when he'd made his case for video stores he'd been met by one of the young Turks aligned with Tommy Vulpo, a fair nonethnic type with an earring, who laid out the ground rules:

1. No force unless absolutely necessary;
2. No targets inside the Toledo city limits;
3. Weapons to be obtained through the organization and nowhere else;
4. A seventy-thirty split in favor of Wild Bill's crew on cash (renegotiated from sixty-forty), with 80 percent of the profits from credit-card slips going to the organization, which would assume responsibility for turning them into cash;
5. In the case of arrest, legal representation to be provided by the organization, so long as none of the other rules had been compromised, and the nature of the part-

nership kept off the record by all defendants.

Wild Bill had balked when Vulpo's man insisted upon recruiting his crew from the available local talent, but had relented upon assurance that no one would be forced on him without his approval, and an agreement pending approval from Vulpo that Mark Twain would be included. Wild Bill had met Mark in the tank in Idaho, where Mark was being held for extradition to Michigan for violating parole. It was his advice that the Midwest was a better place to ply his trade that had eventually decided Wild Bill to come home and take on the responsibilities of clearing the title to the house in Kentucky. Mark in his turn had brought in Donny, a driver who had proven himself under pressure.

Ironically, the only men who had given Wild Bill cause for doubt were the belligerent Carlos and Grinnell, the case man whose slipup in Hilliard had put the whole operation in jeopardy.

In the main, however, he was sanguine. Neither he nor his crew had been identified as yet by the authorities, and the people he answered to in Toledo seemed prepared to absorb the heat. He'd been confident enough about the future to litter the glass-topped table at his elbow with brochures promoting Ohio bookstores and some newspaper sections with ads announcing forthcoming appearances of name authors. Such an event brought in nearly as much as the Friday-night opening of a major Hollywood film at a multiplex.

One or two scores like that and Wild Bill could settle all the liens against the property, sell it for ten times what his father had paid for it in 1960, put the money down on a dude ranch or a resort hotel in either Colorado or New Mexico, and live out his days as a land baron of the old school, craggy and respectable.

Unless, of course, the Uncle Jakey in his blood called.

Wild Bill Berman twirled his outlaw Colt, watching the shadows crawl across Daniel Boone and daydreaming about easy banks, slow trains, and willing women.

TEN

"COLOR GUARD" QUESTIONS
PLAGUE ARTF
— *Columbus Dispatch*

HOMELAND SECURITY PROBES
"COLOR GUARD," TERRORISM LINK
— *Toledo Blade*

PRINE: "COLOR GUARD" BREAK
EXPECTED SOON
— *Cleveland Plain Dealer*

HUE CREW SCREWS BLUES
— *Bowling Green Blast*

Edgar Prine, who for thirty years had taxed the vocabulary of the Ohio press for phrases to describe his demeanor other than the shopworn "poker-faced," "solemn," and "humorless," chuckled as he shuffled through the colorful printouts of recent front pages on the big worktable in the office he used for genuine police business. He held up the last.

"What or who is the *Bowling Green Blast*?"

"Underground student newspaper," Lieutenant McCormick said. "You can't find it except on the Net and maybe scattered all over the floor of the student union. University's been trying to shut it down for a year."

"Find out who wrote this piece and get him credentials. He's the only cherry in a box of stale acorns."

"Give him Wagner's?" Lewis Wagner's byline appeared under the *Dispatch* headline hounding the Armed Robbery Task Force for results.

"No, he's the governor's pup. He'll bark the other way after the election." Prine looked again at the *Blade*. "You been probed by Homeland Security lately?"

"Not a poke. God knows where they got that."

"Whose name we don't take in vain," the captain reminded him. "At least Cleveland knows how to report a press conference. Why do they always use that picture? Makes me look like Mighty Joe Young."

"You swept out the photo editor's cousin when you investigated the CPD for selling evidence from the property room. You're lucky he doesn't slug your name under Hannibal Lecter. Ken Abelard at WTOL was the first to use that 'Color Guard' tag. You'd think the print boys would steal from one of their own."

"Well, you can't wrap your garbage in a TV set. We should've held back the matching-shirts angle. Give 'em a hook and they'll chew each other to pieces to grab at it."

"They didn't get it from us. The guys that put words in Abelard's mouth interviewed witnesses in all four robberies." McCormick brushed at a lapel; Prine didn't need to run a DNA test to determine he'd come there straight from one of his wife's haircuts. "The *Dispatch* jumped a human-interest piece to the inside, about Cy Oliver: Married nineteen years, son killed in a car crash on prom night a couple years back. One of his neighbors said he used to bring her kid Disney videos they'd pulled from the rack; you know, the ones they sell as previously viewed. Nice guy."

Oliver was the manager killed in Hilliard. "He should've stuck with that instead of bringing a gun to work. Civilian heroes screw up the natural order worse than heisters."

"I still think we should pull in Tommy Vulpo. It'd give the fish something fresh to fight over."

"He'd stonewall us, just like at his house. Only this time it'd be all over the media."

In fact, Crazy Joe's crazy son had talked the whole time Prine and McCormick were with him. They'd learned all about his pocket-comb collection, the hazards of bidding against other pocket-comb collectors on eBay, and the general decline in quality in pocket combs manufactured since the 1950s. He'd finished by unlocking a bleached cabinet in his pale study and showing them a sample of his collection, rows and rows of plastic pocket combs, each one identical to all the others. The face he'd shown them whenever they asked about the recent string of video-store robberies was as bland as anything in his fucking bland collection. (McCormick's words, on their way back to Columbus; Prine's own language was as tidy and presentable as the fake office where he addressed Ohio.) They'd heard Joe Vulpo clumping around upstairs the whole time they were interviewing Tommy, but they'd heard enough nutcake babble for one visit and didn't ask to see him.

"Think Tommy really collects pocket combs?" McCormick asked.

"Bras and panties, more like, in his size. He probably boosted the combs off a truck sometime by mistake. He may have hit on the best strategy during questioning: Bore 'em into committing suicide. He's just as looney as he wants to be. If we ever bust him for anything it'll be for dressing up like the world's ugliest woman and scaring old perverts to death at Franklin Park Mall." Prine drummed together the newspaper material and jammed it into a wastebasket already stuffed with faxes and printouts. "What we got on that composite sketch?"

"Department mainframe matched it to a half-dozen mugs on file. I told the geek to forward it to your box."

Prine went to his desk and logged on. "Only six? It looked like anybody's brother-in-law."

"They narrowed it down to noncombatants: front men, forgers, embezzlers. The mob doesn't normally employ heavy-lifters for case work."

The captain scrolled through three rows of front-and-profile photographs, went back, and stopped. "That one's familiar." He pointed.

McCormick leaned over his shoulder. "Sure does. And I know from where."

"Tommy Vulpo's driveway."

The pictures were of one John Grinnell

Benjamin, a Canadian citizen arrested in Detroit in 1995 for conspiring to smuggle unlicensed tobacco products across a state line. Prine clicked onto his file. The manager of a supermarket in Sandusky had identified him as the man who'd arranged to sell him sixty cartons of cigarettes without tax stamps. The manager had been under arrest for the same charge and was offered the opportunity to plead to a lesser offense in return for his cooperation. A bench warrant was issued for Benjamin's arrest based on a partial license-plate number, and he was detained while attempting to cross the Ambassador Bridge into Windsor, where he was a resident. Returned to Ohio to face his accusers, he was booked and printed, held overnight, and released when the supermarket manager failed to pick him out of a lineup. Representing Benjamin on that occasion was an attorney with a firm retained by Joe Vulpo.

"No previous record," Prine said. "Did you get a license number?"

"I sure didn't. Foreign bucket. Toyota? Lexus. Frost green Lexus, this year's or last year's model."

"Put out a BOLO here and in Michigan, and tell the Canadian authorities to check out his address. It's seven years old, but you never know. Creature of habit, still doing business with the same people."

"Hold him on what, driving in Tommy Vulpo's driveway?"

"We can pull him in for questioning."

"Then in comes Tommy's lawyer to jerk him back out on the street. Meanwhile we show our hand."

"It's the only hand we've got. We can lose him in the system for a few days. If he's working for Toledo full-time, maybe he's living in this country. Maybe he forgot to renew his visa, or to apply for one in the first place. Or he never got around to registering as an alien."

"I'm not sure Canadians have to do any of that."

"Check. His record's clean both sides of the cigarette deal. Good case man's got nothing if not anonymity. We can threaten to release his name and mug to the press. These quiet ones are a lot easier to crack than the ones that've had the tour."

McCormick rubbed his nose; trying to erase the marks of the reading glasses he wore in private, Prine guessed. "If he doesn't, we'll be up to our balls in a false-arrest suit."

"Well, we've had those before. We're

past due. It beats sitting around scratching ourselves."

"Not if he turns out not to be our guy. All we know is what we knew seven years ago, that he's Vulpo's man. And we don't even know that. We could both be wrong about who we saw driving that car."

"We've been wrong before, too," Prine said, logging off. "But never both at the same time."

ELEVEN

Among the few who knew how Sunny Wong made most of her cash (of whom Grinnell was one), she was known as "the beast with two fronts."

Outside that circle, the phrase was a mystery. There was nothing remotely beastlike about her five-foot-one, one hundred-pound frame or her fine Asian features, and even those who recognized the tong symbols tattooed from her shoulders to her elbows could not deny they'd been done by almost a dainty hand. But anyone who chanced to see her clubbing frogs in the rural marshes beyond the Cincinnati sprawl was halfway to the answer.

Every weekend during summer, Sunny drove her stove-in Ford Ranger pickup west of suburban Finneytown, put on waders, twisted her waist-length hair up under a Reds cap, and slogged in among the leeches and mosquito wigglers, swinging a sawed-off Tennessee Thumper baseball bat right and left and throwing the stunned amphibians into a five-gallon plastic bucket slung from one shoulder. When the bucket was full, she went back to the truck for another, and when she had a truckload she returned to her house and two acres, dunked the frogs in a mixture of ammonia and formaldehyde, packed them snugly in USPS-approved containers, and shipped them to research laboratories and high-school biology departments throughout the United States.

She charged ninety cents a frog, and averaged fifteen hundred frogs per outing. But this was only the first of her two fronts, the legitimate one.

Her house was a one-story clapboard construction that looked bigger than it was because the broad side faced the street. In fact it was only eighteen feet deep, shallower than a double-wide trailer, and in order to walk from one end to the other, you passed through all the rooms, which were laid out in succession with partitions between and the doors lined up straight; what the low-income residents of an earlier generation, for whom the thought of owning any sort of house had seemed an impossible childhood fantasy, called "shotgun style." Here she lived, and met customers at the door to begin the transactions connected with her second front.

An addition had been built onto the back, the length of the house and nearly as deep. Sunny had filled it with cages and terrariums, which contained some 163 varieties of snakes, turtles, sundry other reptiles, and tarantulas, which she sold to university students, indulgent parents of inquisitive children, certain underworld figures, punk rockers, and professional strippers. The students and children kept the snakes, turtles, and tarantulas as pets, while the punks and strippers used the big snakes almost exclusively onstage. The underworld types favored monitor lizards, rattlesnakes, and gilas for the purpose of intimidating enemies and disloyal friends.

The strippers were Sunny's most consistent customers. She had been one herself, and so she knew which types of python and defanged diamondback were most suitable for exhibition. The exotic dancers respected her opinion and came from as far away as Las Vegas and Miami to make purchases with fistfuls of sweaty singles and five-dollar bills. One had traveled all the way from Newfoundland and paid fifteen thousand dollars cash for an iguana, which she planned to lead around by a leash attached to a jeweled collar; she would then smear her naked body with honey and lie down on the runway while the lizard licked her clean with its long forked tongue. (Sunny had recommended nettle honey. Iguanas have acrid tastes.)

None of these customers, it should be pointed out, possessed a permit to keep an exotic pet, and in many cases the animals were protected and private ownership was prohibited. This was of no concern to Sunny, who had neither a permit to sell exotic animals nor a zoning variance to conduct any sort of business in a residential neighborhood. She had been cited for the latter many times, had paid fines, and suspended operation for six months during the term of a reform mayor, setting up again after the next election turned him out of office as they always did. More serious were the threats of an investigation from the Department of Natural Resources in Columbus, the likelihood of a raid, and possible prison time for innumerable violations of the state conservation law.

However, Sunny Wong was content to go on as she had for years, paying certain officials to deflect official attention. Should that procedure fail, she could cash out her legitimate investments and hire a sharp legal firm to delay her case for months or years or however long it took for the tide to turn in the capital. Or for the present administration to lose interest in a case that never came to court or promised a single vote. She could afford to be content. As lucrative as it was, the illegal trade in *fauna exotica* was merely a front for her traffic in undocumented firearms.

The cages and glass tanks in her back room stood atop a shallow underground vault built of concrete and lined with zinc, containing five million dollars (retail) in automatic rifles, semiautomatic pistols, revolvers, and cases of unissued grenade launchers from Desert Storm, packed in cosmoline and moisture-resistant Styrofoam peanuts. Under a six-foot pile of manure certain to discourage the most fanatic searcher, accessed by a rotating panel that moved the pile aside in a body, were crates and boxes of brass and stainless-steel cartridges, including explosive rounds outlawed in every country except North Korea, where they had been obtained by American mercenaries who knew where all the markets were in the U.S. Somewhere — Sunny had told someone she thought they were stored in an airtight Mylar case in a gila burrow with a false bottom — a six-pack of antipersonnel bombs resembling Osage oranges waited to turn human beings inside out; she really needed to take inventory, she said, she'd had them at least five years and they were probably unstable. She may have been teasing, but with the beast with two fronts you were never sure.

She sold these items only to people she'd done business with before or who could provide verifiable references. A stranger who wandered in asking to see the "real inventory" got the dumb-Chinee look and an offer to see the komodo dragon, which if it weren't stuffed would be the most valuable item in the menagerie, two hundred thousand on the current black market. Or if she had the cramps she would simply show him the baseball bat she used on frogs. No one in authority, not ATF or the Bureau or the Cincinnati police, knew she was the largest dealer in illicit guns in the Midwest. The Ohio Department of Natural Resources would consider that justice had been served once she was arrested and convicted for the import and sale of unlicensed lizards and related misdemeanors. Only a genius or an idiot would suspect her illegal operation of being a front for one even more illegal.

It would have puzzled — and alarmed — Tommy Vulpo to learn that Ben Grinnell was in on Finneytown's best-kept secret. This was no accident. When he first came to work for the Toledo crime family, Grinnell had decided it was in his best interest not to disclose all his qualifications.

Tommy, and before him Joe, the Iron Boss, had mistaken him for the retiring, nonviolent type. It wasn't uncommon for a man with street-soldier experience to possess good manners and an education, but he was in every other way unremarkable to the point of boredom. He was the kind of guest you introduced someone to at a cocktail party in order to excuse yourself from the ordeal of holding a conversation with him. The aridness of his personality was so well established that it was almost no longer an act. It had quite certainly kept him out of harm's way, which was a position he knew firsthand and loathed, not because of physical danger, but because when the heat turned up it was those who occupied it who were thrown into the flames. He was regarded on the same level with a bookkeeper or a file clerk — someone whose skills were useful, but whose criminal knowledge was as limited as his personal magnetism. Had Tommy suspected the truth, he might have put his case man in charge of something worse than procuring weapons, such as dismemberment and burial of disloyal employees. Grinnell was no stranger to that detail, nor to most others. He was, in fact, an anomaly in the highly specialized world of organized crime, post–Murder, Incorporated: a jack-of-all-trades.

As he pulled into the gravel bed that served as Sunny Wong's front yard, he suspected he was under surveillance. That's why he'd rented an SUV, driven it through a couple of mud holes, and put on ragged Carhartt overalls and a dime-store adjustable baseball cap, the local uniform. Anyone studying the snapshots or videotape later would assume he'd come to buy a crocodile. The license-plate number would only trace back to the agency, which had recorded the transaction under the false name on the driver's license, through one of a tangle of legitimate corporations that might lead back to Joe Vulpo after two years of research. For good measure he walked stoop-shouldered, but denied himself the flamboyant indulgence of a limp. In his amateur theatrical days he'd been a bit of a ham, but his longest-running role to date was the one he'd been playing for years.

A woolly mongrel banged to the end of

its chain, barking and snarling, as he walked past. The dog — collie, shepherd, and something worse — kept up its protest until the door opened and Sunny yelled. It sank onto its haunches and reached back to worry a clump of hair off its hip. Great gray patches of skin showed where the dog had shed.

Without a word, the proprietress held open the door for the visitor to enter. She shut it and hurled herself at Grinnell.

He had to catch her to keep from being thrown against the door. Her tongue filled his mouth, a squirming thing like one of her snakes, but far warmer.

When at last it was out of the way of his own, Grinnell said, "I wasn't sure you'd remember."

"Remember who? I thought you came to read the meter. Nobody's laid me in weeks."

Inches apart as their faces were, he saw the first lines of age in her bisquelike features. She was thirty-five, but made up and dressed for town, she had to show ID to buy cigarettes. He could tell, holding her, she wasn't wearing a bra under her sleeveless boy's undershirt. She smelled of sweat and turtle food.

"A lot's happened since we saw each other," he said.

She looked from one eye to the other, frowned. Then she uncoiled her legs from around his waist and hopped to the floor. Apart from the undershirt she had on camouflage cargo pants and black rubber galoshes. Her nipples poked through thin white cotton. "You went and got yourself hitched. Who is she? I'll send her a rhinoceros viper as a wedding present."

"No one gets hitched anymore. *You* told me that. Anyway, you're not jealous. What happened to that fat sheriff's deputy?"

"He shot a little kid and took early retirement. I didn't want him sitting around the house scaring away customers. Where you been, John? I heard you were running a casino in Windsor."

"That was a silent partnership. I sold out. We couldn't compete with the Indians across the river. They can break all the gaming laws and answer to no one but the tribal council, and guess who runs the casinos? Also, it's not John anymore. It's Ben Grinnell. I made some changes when I became a citizen."

"U.S.? What the hell for?"

"I couldn't afford the General Service Tax."

"Bullshit. Since when do you pay taxes?"

"Since I moved here. I've got nobody in

Canada. I think my brother's in Afghanistan. Last I heard he was a major in the Canadian Army."

"Next you'll tell me you've gone square."

"Too risky. I'm here on business, as a matter of fact."

She stepped in close, groped him from neck to waist, cupped his genitals.

"I'm not wired," he said.

She stepped back. "I didn't see you so long. A lot can happen."

"I said that."

She smiled. She had beautiful teeth. She'd told him that when she was a stripper she'd cleared more tips than any of the other girls because she was the only one who didn't scowl all the way through her act. "Or look bored," she'd added. "That's worse. Men are the same all over. They want to think it's your first time. It's worth a hundred extra bucks a night if you can fake a blush."

What she said now was, "I can always count on you, John. Almost everyone I know's in some kind of federal program, wearing a wire or walking around Gopher Shit, Nebraska, telling people their name's Joe Doakes. Ratting out their whole world, just to stay out of the can."

"What's the difference?"

"Spoken like someone who's never been inside."

"Have you?"

"Five hours, when they raided the club for violating the liquor laws. Only dumb fucks do stone time."

"I'll remind you of that when you're in Marion. They're watching you from the house across the street. Curtains drawn in only one window, with a two-inch gap for the lens to see through."

"That's just State. They want to keep box turtles out of the hands of children. Same old shit, John. They're trying some poor schmuck in Michigan for killing a rattlesnake. They're protected in Lansing. Meanwhile a guy can beat his ex-girlfriend half to death in Detroit, do his five hours, and come back to finish the job."

"It's still Ben, not John. Try to remember that."

"What's the matter, scared of your past?"

"Paralyzed. I'm not even supposed to know you exist. When they ask me where the stuff came from, I'm going to have to say I asked around."

"What stuff's that? I club frogs." She was still grinning.

"How's business?"

"They keep me hopping. What you need?"

"Shotgun and two sidearms. Sig Sauer nine-millimeters, if you have them."

She patted back a yawn. "I got Sigs up the ass. You can get a Sig on the street; ask any of those boys in Cinci, leaning on their Chevies smoking Marlboros. Ask me something hard. I just got in a shipment of fifty-mag S-and-W's. The army can't get 'em, but they don't have my contacts."

"The people I'm buying for aren't hunting elephants. I need virgin stock, not those been-around pieces you get from the boys in Cincinnati. Men are the same all over. They want to think it's the first time."

She laughed. She had a tinkly giggle, the only thing about her that was remotely Asian, apart from her looks. "Let's go back into inventory."

He followed her through a small living room furnished in vintage redneck — crushed velour and duck-decoy lamps — to a door that looked like an ordinary hollow-core, but that he remembered contained a slab of case-hardened steel, impossible to kick down or ram through, and waited while she unlocked it from a ring of keys she took from one of the many pockets in her cargo pants. When she opened it, the stench of manure and weapons-grade disinfectant struck him in the face like a frying pan. An alarm sounded, high-pitched and impatient. He waited again while she punched out an eleven-digit code on a keypad in the door frame. The noise stopped.

Fluorescent tubes in troughs mounted on the ceiling shed pale light on rows of cages and glass tanks. They sheltered a hundred or more varieties of reptile, insect, and arachnid, at least twice as many as the last time Grinnell had visited. The price of the stock connected with her second front would be far more than the house and property were worth. There was a handsome living there, but she seemed to prefer the heightened risk involved with her real enterprise. He suspected their attraction for each other lay in the mutual lives of deception they led. Certainly Sunny Wong was the only person he'd known who had seen through the bland mask he wore for the world.

She worked a hidden catch and slid open a shallow drawer in the bottom of a mesh cage. A Goliath beetle the size of a kitten watched her from its bamboo perch on the other side of the mesh. The drawer had been designed to collect droppings for easy disposal, but she'd lined it with tarnish-resistant gray plush. Four nickel-plated semiautomatic pistols lay there side by side, identical and shining with oil. Sunny selected one, produced a chamois cloth from another pocket, and wiped it off expertly.

"I slather it on," she said, twisting one corner and working it between the trigger and the back of the trigger guard. "It's easier to remove than cosmoline and the compartment's airtight. Doesn't collect dust." She offered him the butt.

He took the weapon, sprang loose the magazine, saw it was empty, worked the slide to inspect the empty chamber, and snapped everything back together. He did all this in less time than it took to describe; but then an IRA assassin had taught him how to disassemble and reassemble a Swedish assault rifle blindfolded. It was a cheap parlor trick, with almost no practical application outside a training camp, but Grinnell's dexterity had impressed the handful of people who had witnessed it. All except Sunny Wong, who busied herself stroking the side of the cage with an index finger to make sure the beetle hadn't expired on its perch. The insect responded by twitching its enormous mandibles.

Grinnell returned the pistol. "Sack it up and wipe off another. What about the shotgun? Autoloader, twelve-gauge."

"Imported or domestic?" She lay the Sig Sauer on top of the cage and picked up its neighbor, still holding the chamois in her other hand.

"The man favors Franchis."

"Who doesn't? That's a back order. Take a week."

"I never knew you to run short on anything."

"Ever since *The Godfather* came out on DVD I can't keep 'em in stock. Everyone wants to be Fabrizio: 'Hey, Joe, take me to America!' " She had the worst Italian accent west of Hong Kong.

"Beretta, then. He won't wait a week."

"I can let you have a trap model for a thousand. Recoil pad, Monte Carlo stock. Pletty rittle piece." Her pidgin English was a microscopic improvement.

"No stock. Pistol grip."

"I got one. Have to move the cottonmouths to get to it. I hate those 'mouths. They remind me of my venerated grandfather."

"Tong?"

She shook her head. "Headwaiter at

the Peking Duck in Chillicothe. That's p-e-e-king; the logo on the menu's a duck looking at you between its fingers."

"Ducks have fingers?"

"Eight-fifty for the Beretta," she said. "Sixteen hundred for the two Sigs. You won't find a better deal."

"I'm not looking for one. It's not my money."

"What do you spend your money on? No arrests or lawyers, you must have a pile."

"Now that you mention it," he said.

She blinked. He never gave confidences.

"I need a personal arm."

She laid the Sig Sauer next to the other, looked up at him, and smiled. "John, John," she said. "You backslider."

TWELVE

> Even the boys in Toledo don't know everything that's here. Had to spread mustard pretty high up the fence to get it. We'll settle later.

The note clipped to the contents of the thick nine-by-twelve envelope was written in Loyal Dorfman's backward-leaning hand, in blue ballpoint on plain copy paper, without greeting or signature. A quick glance inside while the desk clerk in the hotel in Toledo had been printing out Macklin's bill showed photographs, a facsimile of an arrest report, and page after page of close type. The clerk had handed him the envelope while Laurie brought the car under the canopy for loading. He'd stuffed the envelope into an overnight case to read later. There'd been no sense telling her about it until he knew what it contained.

Now, sitting on the bed in their room at the Best Western in Myrtle, he waited until he heard water running in the tub, then dumped the faxed and photocopied material out onto the spread. From instinct he went to the pictures first. There were front-and-profile mugs of a younger, somewhat leaner Grinnell with longer hair, and more recent candid shots taken with a long lens of him crossing a broad street on foot, getting into a cab, talking on a sidewalk with someone whom Macklin didn't recognize, but whose stocky build, Hawaiian shirt worn tail out, black-black sunglasses, and mullet haircut screamed mid-level mob. There were a lot of pictures involving the man in the Hawaiian shirt, and only three or four of Grinnell alone, indicating he was not the focus of the surveillance. Whoever had taken the photos had followed him to his cab after the meeting, recording visual details for further investigation.

The typewritten material had been obtained from reports by the Justice Department, Immigration, the Department of State, and sealed documents provided by confidential informants whose names had been blacked out; some of the pages had been nearly obliterated by some civil servant whose job consisted of drawing laundry markers through any passages of a personal nature. Reading between the inked-out sections, Macklin learned that his mother-in-law's — what, paramour? — was a native Canadian named John Grinnell Benjamin, a distant relative on his mother's side of George Bird Grinnell, the nineteenth-century anthropologist whose two-volume study of the Cheyenne Indians was still in print. He was the second son of a history professor at the University of Toronto. His father had died when John was three. The older son, Theodore, was a career officer in the Canadian Army. Whoever had compiled that part of the report presumed that their elderly mother was supported by money sent by both sons; the upscale assisted-living community where she lived in North York would not be satisfied with a university widow's pension, and anything a simple military officer could contribute would scarcely have been adequate.

The younger Benjamin had abandoned his Christian name and transposed his middle and surnames four years earlier, when he'd applied for U.S. citizenship. Because his only brush with the law on either side of the border was a prior arrest for trafficking in contraband cigarettes — a charge dropped later for lack of evidence — his application had been accepted. Such papers were reviewed daily by the ton; examiners couldn't be expected to run every piece of information to ground, and in any case much of the data in Macklin's hands was based on speculation and hearsay. Benjamin Grinnell had stood in a crowd at the federal courthouse in Detroit, raised his right hand, and sworn allegiance to the United States of America. John Grinnell Benjamin was a suspected associate of Toronto's oldest crime family — an organization that had predated the American Revolution, grown fat hiring out to the Crown to break the French blockade and supply British troops in the field — and a liaison between the English-speaking syndicate and the Frontenac brothers in Quebec, whom the authorities in Montreal had been trying to convict for extortion and murder since the 1960s. Jacques and Louis Frontenac had made a fortune providing false identification and transportation for Americans fleeing the draft during Vietnam, and lately had established a monopoloy on the trade in cheap prescription medicines across the international border. Much blood had been shed in this pursuit, and some investigators in Ottawa were convinced that Benjamin had been directly involved. Wiretaps in the Frontenac offices in Mont-Royal had recorded more than a hundred references to someone named "Long John" during a particularly bloody three-week period when most of the brothers' competitors retired from the field.

None of it was evidence, and the information on the American side was even sketchier. Dorfman's Ohio sources reported casual acquaintanceship with Ben Grinnell in connection with several interests shared with the Vulpo family in Toledo. So far even the local authorities were unaware he existed, and were they privy to the material spread out on the bed Macklin shared with Laurie, they wouldn't have enough to obtain a warrant for his arrest. But Macklin didn't need a warrant to identify a predator by the pack it traveled with.

Why Grinnell should have taken up with Pamela Ziegenthaler, a divorced bookstore manager in a place like Myrtle, was the real question. It became a little less impenetrable when he figured in the fact that Pamela's daughter was married to a former predator named Macklin. Coincidence was something he couldn't rule out right away; but he only believed in it so far as he accepted the existence of an unseen God. Before accepting the whim of Providence he had first to eliminate all the things of this world.

Confirming his suspicions neither elated nor satisfied him. It just made him tired. He'd spent two years traveling in a straight line in search of a normal life and it had led him clear around the world and back to where he'd started.

The realtor's name was Linda, a large woman with a pretty face who wore a corsage the size of a dinner plate on one shoulder to play down her linebacker's build in the orange company blazer. She greeted Peter and Laurie in the common room that in Laurie's youth had been the front of Theisiger's Confectionery and held open the door of her office for them to enter. It was a windowless room paneled in weathered barnwood, with a desk, chairs, computer, a credenza piled with brochures, and an acrylic portrait of Linda, her husband, and three children painted from a photograph and framed on the wall behind the desk. All wore cheesy smiles overlaid with appliance white, and Laurie had the sudden giddy thought that under a black light all those straightened and bonded teeth would glow like the Cheshire cat's. Peter had noticed the portrait as well, but as usual she couldn't guess what he was thinking. If he decided to surprise her by having something like that done from their wedding picture, she sensed a fight.

When they were all seated, Linda asked them how they were enjoying their stay in Myrtle.

"We're just back," Laurie said. "We were in Toledo overnight."

"Did you take in the botanical garden? I make it a point to go there twice a year. It changes that often. I'm an amateur horticulturist." She turned her head slightly and sniffed at her corsage. It looked as if it would squirt water when she squeezed a bulb.

"My mother took me there when I was eight. I sneezed the whole time. I think it was the insecticide."

"I believe in organic gardening myself. For every pest, nature provides a bigger one with a greater appetite. So you've reached a decision?" Her left eye twitched when she lifted her brows.

Peter spoke up. "You said three-sixty, I think."

Linda swiveled toward her computer and rattled some keys. "Yes. A very good price in today's market. There are several developments planned in the neighborhood. If you decide to sell, you could double your investment in two years."

Laurie said, "We don't intend to sell it. We're going to raise our children there."

"You're expecting? Congratulations! The schools —"

"We're expecting to expect." She squeezed Peter's hand beneath the top of the desk. "I grew up on that property and we plan to grow old on it."

"That's very refreshing. So many people are afraid to set down roots. The owners are willing to enter into a five-year land contract, if you can put a hundred thousand down. What's the name of your financial institution?"

Peter drew his checkbook out of his inside breast pocket. "It's on the check."

They'd planned to celebrate by having a picnic in the front yard of the farmhouse. All the way to the realtor's, Laurie had been suggesting supplies: tablecloth, bottle of wine, bread and sliced turkey for sandwiches. She'd spotted a large convenience store that sold package liquor on the site of the old cider mill, and Macklin drove back that direction. But something else was on her mind now, he could tell, and he had to wait until he stopped for a traffic light before she spoke.

"Just like that, you draw up a check for a hundred thousand dollars."

"There's a little more to it. I'll have to do a telephone transfer so it won't bounce."

"We don't have that much in savings."

He hesitated. "It's a different account."

"There's another account?"

"There are three, not counting a safe deposit box in Detroit."

The light changed. When they were moving again she said, "More secrets?"

"I opened several after I sold the camera stores. I told you about them when we were engaged. You were too starry-eyed to pay attention."

"I guess the honeymoon wiped them out of my mind. You never said how much was in them."

"Are you asking me how much money we have?"

Another block slid past. Macklin saw inflatable wading pools, a soccer ball resting against a flower bed bordered with whitewashed stones, an elaborate gym set, no children. UV rays, the West Nile virus, and child abductions leading off every news report had emptied the front yards and sentenced a generation to life in front of computers and SpongeBob Squarepants.

"Yes."

"Well, you know about the hundred thousand, which we don't have anymore as of twenty minutes ago. There's a little over sixty thousand in Switzerland. It's been months since I checked Andorra and the Caymans, but figuring interest —"

"Are we millionaires?"

"Technically; but what's that? If your mother cashed everything out tomorrow, she'd be too. There's a long way between a million and Bill Gates."

"How much of it is blood money?"

"Not much. You know what I took from Maggiore. I earned that for all the times he tried to kill me. The rest came when I sold the stores."

"That was a front, you said."

"Some fronts have been known to pay better than what they're fronting for. Toward the end I think I was spending more time running the stores than —"

"Killing people."

He turned a corner. A laser-tag facility occupied an immaculate building standing on an entire city block, with a GRAND OPENING banner swagged across the front. That was where the kids went when they weren't watching TV or interacting with Lara Croft, running down halls and shooting at one another. He was gladder than ever he'd left the life when he had. In ten years the competition was going to be fierce.

He said, "It might interest you to know I sometimes went a year or two at a time without killing anyone. Gang wars are risky and expensive. They eat up a lot of good men and draw too much attention. And most of the local branches handle their own mop-up. There were people on the inside who thought I was just Mike Boniface's errand boy. It's not like the Old West. I wouldn't have lasted half as long as I did if I had a reputation."

"What happened to all the money you made running errands?"

"Most of it went into the house in Southfield. Then there was Roger's tuition, and putting clothes on Donna's back. The rest went to her in the settlement."

"She must be the richest divorcée in Southfield."

"I'm not the Man with the Golden Gun. The pay was good but I had three neighbors who were doing better than me shuffling papers and taking meetings. Mike didn't believe in spoiling his employees."

"Then why didn't you quit?" Her voice broke.

"I did."

She said nothing until he slowed down to turn into the convenience store parking lot. "Keep going."

He flipped off the indicator. "What about our picnic?"

"I'm not hungry."

"Where to, then, your mother's?"

"She's at the bookstore. I don't feel like browsing either. Let's just drive around for a while, okay? Look at the changes."

"Are you mad at me?"

"No."

He made a decision. She was upset, even if not directly at him. He might as well take her the rest of the way.

"There's an envelope in the backseat. I didn't want to tell you about it until after the picnic."

She looked, reached back between the seats, and hoisted it onto her lap. "What's in it?"

"Benjamin Grinnell."

THIRTEEN

Wild Bill, who at eighteen had spent a bad first week in Colorado adjusting to the elevation, had learned the principles of hydration. Keeping the tissues sluiced down prevented any manner of complaints, and at the risk of ridicule from some of his less enlightened companions he never went anywhere without his own supply of water. On a blistering afternoon like the one he was spending on Exit 39 in Forest Park, he could have bathed in the stuff and still had enough left over to turn a profit if he'd cared to sell it. He'd sure have done better business than selling flowers.

He drank off all but a cupful of his fifth plastic bottle and sprinkled the rest over the inventory: the sorriest-looking bunch of cheap posies he'd seen all in one place, but he'd managed to sell three bouquets in an hour at five bucks a pop. Every motorist who'd forked over was male, with the same worried look. They'd each had a fight with the wife over the telephone from work and had steered toward his hand-lettered sign on their way down the ramp like a lost ship's captain making for dry land. Wild Bill wondered if the women they'd married were dumb enough to accept a wilted bunch of stems smelling of exhaust fumes in lieu of a night on the town.

Everything smelled of exhaust. Even the water had a distinct aftertaste of regular unleaded.

He spotted Grinnell soon after he turned off the expressway, even though he was driving one of his rented brown paper bags on wheels. The man always drove with his seat pushed close to the dash and both hands on the wheel; Wild Bill had seen him often enough circling parking lots where he and the others were parked before a job, and he prided himself on his ability to observe and recognize driving styles, the way an old-time cowboy knew an acquaintance was approaching by his posture in the saddle.

Grinnell cruised the beige SUV to a stop, waited for the dust to drift past, and powered down the window. "Is this what you do when you're not sticking people up?"

"I gave the guy a fifty to take the afternoon off. That's more'n he makes in a weekend. What you dressed up for, a hill-billy wedding?" Grinnell was wearing ragged Carhartt overalls, in sharp contrast to his indoor personality.

"Never mind that. Where do you want me to make delivery?"

"Right here. I didn't set this up to put FTD out of business."

The man behind the wheel looked around. A towering car transporter thundered down the ramp huffing its air brakes and swept around Wild Bill, lifting his long hair and snatching petals off the bunch of flowers he was holding. The trailer was loaded with new Hondas. "In broad daylight?"

"I never knew what that meant," Wild Bill said. "I never saw no narrow daylight."

"We might as well do this in front of the State House. There are underground garages."

"I don't like tight spaces. They'll just think you're delivering more flowers."

Grinnell drummed his fingers on the steering wheel. Then he put the SUV in park, got out, and unlocked the back hatch. A Ford Escort ticked past as he took out the bundle wrapped in a black garbage bag and laid it in Wild Bill's arms. The driver glanced at them briefly, then went on to the stop sign at the end of the ramp.

Wild Bill groped at the long object in the sack. “Franchi?”

“Beretta.”

“Shit.”

“It’s what I could get. I got you the Sigs and boxes of shells. Try not to use them on anyone this time.”

“I should let myself get shot full of holes by some prick manager with his first piece.”

“Well, I wasn’t there.”

“Goddamn right you wasn’t. You wasn’t there when you *was* there.”

Grinnell’s face was unreadable. Wild Bill felt the tension going out of his own. “They ream you out in Toledo?”

“Get the package out of sight.” An official-looking vehicle left the expressway heading down the ramp.

Wild Bill strode over to the hatchback he’d stolen in Lexington and laid the bundle in the cargo compartment. The official-looking vehicle was a white van belonging to the Ohio Parks Department. It paused at the stop sign and turned left.

“How much I owe you?”

Grinnell shook his head. “We’re still providing the weapons. We’ll take it out of the back end like always.”

"That's where I been taking it my whole life." Wild Bill spat out his snuff.

"When do you go again?"

"Next Saturday."

"Where?"

"Want some flowers?" Wild Bill picked up the bunch he'd set aside to accept the package.

Grinnell took it. Wrapped around the stems, secured with a twist of wire, was a page from the Book section of the *Toledo Blade*. He worried it loose, tearing it. An asterisk was scratched in blue ink in the corner of a quarter-page advertisement. He skimmed through it without changing expression.

"Too chancy," he said. "There's bound to be security, maybe even police."

"Small-town cops. They're not much better than store security. What you do is you contain them early. That's Mark's department."

"Famous writers attract long lines. If there's shooting, you'll be wading through corpses. You got a pass in Hilliard, but if it happens again, you're on your own. You know the terms of the arrangement."

"We'll hit the place just before they lock the doors. They'll have the crowd cleared out by then. I checked out a couple of big bookstores in Cinci after I saw the ad. They got his books set up in big displays in front, and stacked up behind 'em to your knees. They're shooting a picture with Kevin Spacey or somebody out of this *Love Song* thing; I saw it on *E.T.* This'll be like hitting three video stores all at once."

Grinnell stuffed the torn sheet back under the wire and smacked the bunch of flowers against Wild Bill's stomach. "I won't case it."

Wild Bill took the flowers. "You're in and out before the shindig winds down. We go in after, just like always. You won't get no blood on your shoes."

"Not any you can see. Why do you think I'm delivering guns now? One more blowup and I'll be cleaning Tommy Vulpo's swimming pool. Or under it."

"Scared?"

"You should be too. I was the goat last time. If Myrtle goes down the same way, he'll cut his losses and feed us all to the hogs. His people get quicker results than the state police."

"Well, we don't need an outside case man. Mark or I could do what you do. You can sit it out and you won't have to shit your pants."

"If I'm out, so's Toledo. You can get

guns anywhere, but if you go ahead without a green light, Myrtle will be the last thing you ever did."

"I'm thinking that anyway. After Saturday night I'll have my stake."

"You're counting plenty on there being a Saturday night."

Wild Bill grinned his gunfighter's grin. "You going to run tell Daddy?"

"Carlos is Vulpo's property. Ask *him* what happens when you work outside the organization."

"All he ever done was bitch anyway. I'm thinking Mark and Donny and I can handle a bunch of bookworms."

"We're through talking, then."

"I think you ain't scared of Tommy," Wild Bill said. "That ad don't say Myrtle. It says the Breakfront Mall, forty minutes southwest of Toledo off of twenty-four. You can drive past a little shit place like Myrtle every day and never know its name. Unless it's your hole in the wall."

Grinnell walked back to his SUV and got in. A piece of gravel clipped Wild Bill's pants leg as he pulled off the shoulder. It was the first time Wild Bill had managed to put a gaffe in that cold fish.

FOURTEEN

Grinnell drove over the overpass and got back on 275 heading back to Miamitown, where he'd left his Lexus and rented the SUV. Stopped in a construction-zone bottleneck, he reached down and slid out the box he'd put under the front seat, just to remind himself not to leave it behind when he switched vehicles, then slid it back. It contained the Browning BDA he'd bought from Sunny Wong: a flat, compact piece that concealed easily and packed a 9mm wallop, just enough to stop a man without passing through him and hitting a citizen, a hard charge to duck even if he had the Vulpos behind him. Dead bystanders seldom went to their graves unaccompanied.

His hand shook a little when he returned it to the steering wheel. Wild Bill didn't frighten him and neither did Tommy Vulpo, when it came down to it, but he'd spent a long time setting up a safe haven in Myrtle and if it got around he'd be on the run. The fugitive life was repellent to him:

an endless cycle of gasoline and rest stops and six-hour stays in anonymous motels and no progress being made.

He and the damned cowboy had one thing in common, a desire to make their boodle and cash out. In Wild Bill's case it was most likely the usual dreary plan, to retire to some bucolic and probably nonexistent village in Mexico or some other place with palm trees and unlimited opportunities for fornication, or to move on to bigger and better scores with less risk, set himself up as Tommy Vulpo Lite. Grinnell just wanted to be let alone. He'd had his fill of the bandit life, gotten his revenge on a remote father who'd expired at seventy in the bed of a female undergraduate when Grinnell was three, and burned off all his adolescent rage against the universe long ago. For a time he'd been contented to remain a semi-uninvolved specialist, identifying potential problems without having to offer a solution or put it in practice, but that situation had begun to sour long before Hilliard.

Pamela Ziegenthaler was a vain, petty woman, who didn't respect him any more than she appreciated her bright, beautiful daughter, but they were compatible in bed and she didn't ask him questions about his work. She was also respectable, and as boring to be around as he tried to be himself. She was his tropical retreat, made up of equal parts security and monotony. Wild Bill would call her a hole in the wall. But Wild Bill and Tommy Vulpo couldn't know about her.

He missed the clear-cut days when a case man was a case man, a button a button, a trafficker in contraband that and nothing else. Now it was all a muddle. When an efficient criminal organization started counting pennies — blurring the lines like any struggling legitimate corporation — mistakes were made, and it was never the people up top who paid for them. If this was midlife crisis, then he shared it with the entire system. And there was only one way to go from middle life.

As if that weren't enough to concern him, he had grave doubts about Pamela's new son-in-law. Peter Macklin struck him as someone who was putting on the same act he was. A quiet man by necessity, Grinnell distrusted other quiet men. When a man wasn't talking he was thinking, and a thought unexpressed could be as dangerous as a concealed weapon. A braggart wore it on his hip for all to see.

There was something else about Macklin

too; an aura, if one wanted to be mystical about it. It was rare, but he'd seen it in others. It put him on his guard as it didn't with characters like Tommy Vulpo and Wild Bill. He could trust them not to be trusted, and when dealing with them could figure his play several moves ahead. He was fairly certain that Macklin had done the same with him over dinner in the restaurant. Grinnell suspected he'd been overplaying his own part, embarrassing even Pamela with his tedious conversation; but Macklin's eyes had never left his, as if he were enthralled with all the gray details of the life of a glorified traveling salesman. No one was as dull as all that. And even if he were, he would never hold the interest of someone like Laurie, a woman whose mature beauty belied her years, whose flashes of intelligence startled even her self-obsessed mother.

The mother distrusted Macklin as well. In her case, it was for most of the same petty reasons that inspired mother-in-law jokes. Later that evening, she'd hinted that Grinnell, with his scattered business acquaintances, might ask around about a Peter Macklin who claimed to have retired from the retail camera business, as if everyone in sales and marketing knew everyone else in that line. Grinnell had been vague in his response. If the man was as dangerous as he seemed, he could find out fairly quickly, although not by asking the people Pamela expected him to. But he was afraid to ask. He wondered if Macklin had been sent to observe him or worse, and if the people behind him caught on that Grinnell was wise, it might force their hand.

So Macklin could wait. The first order of business was to prevent Wild Bill and his crew from robbing Pamela's store next Saturday. But even as he formed that conclusion, Grinnell rejected it. It would mean going to Tommy Vulpo, who would want to know why it was important to him. Tommy was as crazy as old Joe — maybe crazier, having gotten his start earlier in life — but he was no fool, and would see through any complaint that the plan was too dangerous. Grinnell's opposition alone would be enough to attract attention to his hideaway.

No, he would have to accept the assignment to case the bookstore as if the job were no different from all the others. Unlike all the others, he would have to remain on the premises and prevent it from becoming another Hilliard. He was glad he'd trusted his instincts and bought the BDA.

Traffic resumed moving. He drove on to Miamitown and the agency where he'd rented the cumbersome thing he was driving. He'd parked the Lexus in front of a dry cleaner's in the adjoining strip mall. He found a slot next to the other returns and was about to get out when he took a second look at the parking lot next door.

Near the end of the strip, the city had erected a bus stop, shielded by Plexiglas on three sides, with a bench for passengers to rest. A man in a baseball cap and a T-shirt with Chief Wahoo rampant on a field of red sat at one end, reading the *Inquirer.* At the other end sat a stout, elderly woman with a grocery sack on her lap. As Grinnell watched, a city bus slid in front of the stop and coughed its air brakes. It stood still for a full minute, then coughed again and bore away its passengers. The man in the baseball cap remained sitting on the bench. One leg of his blue jeans bulged above the ankle.

Grinnell turned his attention to a public telephone mounted in front of a pet shop two doors down from the dry cleaner, where another man, thickset and balding, stood with one arm resting on the ledge beneath the telephone and the receiver to his ear. He wore his shirttail out over his slacks.

That was enough for Grinnell, but just to make sure he started the SUV and drove around the block. A gray Ford Crown Victoria sedan with whip antennas and a Columbus plate stood unoccupied in a fifteen-minute loading zone on the street that ran parallel to the dry cleaner's. He accelerated and went on to 75 North. He couldn't allow himself to be apprehended with an unregistered pistol in his possession, but if the state police knew his car they also knew his address in Toledo. He might as well go home and wait for them.

Picnic or no, Macklin and Laurie came to the sudden and simultaneous conclusion they were starving. They turned into a Cracker Barrel at high tide, got their names in, and browsed among the novelty clocks, T-shirts, cookie jars, and tins of overpriced toffee in the gift shop until a table opened up. He excused himself to use the men's room. On his way back into the dining room he stopped at the pay telephone, dialed a number from memory, and spoke with the man who answered for two minutes.

As he returned to the table, Laurie collapsed the antenna on her cell telephone.

"Your mother?" He sat down. A weathered crosscut saw hung on the latticework wall beside them.

"I got her answering machine. She must be on her way home from the store."

"Leave a message?"

"I said I had something important to talk about. I left the number."

"When she calls back, tell her you forgot what time we're expected at the autograph party."

"That's not —"

"Now isn't the time to tell her about Grinnell. She'll ask him if it's true."

"He'll deny it, of course. Lying isn't anything to a criminal."

She dropped her voice to a whisper on the last part. A waitress had appeared at their table, eighteen and plump. Laurie and Macklin glanced at their menus. They ordered coffee, chicken-fried chicken, and roast beef. The waitress trundled off.

Macklin said, "We just found out who he is. We don't know who he represents or why he's with your mother. If he finds out we're on to him, we'll never know."

"But if it scares him away —"

"You saw what was in the envelope."

She nodded. "Okay, so he doesn't scare.

Do you think he'll hurt my mother?"

"He doesn't have a history of violence."

"Every history has to start somewhere."

"It wasn't your mother I was talking about. She runs a bookstore. The only enemies she's likely to make are people who paid too much for Harry Potter."

"There are times when I've thought I could kill her myself." She hesitated. "You know I didn't mean that."

"She's a difficult woman. I'll stack up my enemies against hers any day."

"You think it's you they're after?"

"I have to play the odds. So far as I know the Vulpos were never especially friendly with Carlo Maggiore, but they represent the same institution. And then you never know whose toes you're stepping on when you fill a work order."

"Kill a man, you mean."

Their coffee came. When they were alone again he said, "If it's me he's after, getting caught out might force him to act, or force whoever he's spotting for. He's a case man as a rule. As long as he doesn't know we know what he is, we've got an advantage."

"Are you going to kill him?"

The restaurant was packed, with the usual assortment of lively conversants and unruly children. In the din of voices, flatware, and crockery, the couple could have been planning a terrorist act in a normal tone of voice without being overheard.

"You've got killing on the brain," he said. "It's not the only way."

"It's your way. Who did you call?"

He smiled, without humor. "If you can hear through walls, how come you ask so many questions?"

"We've been married a year. You never take more than four minutes to use the bathroom."

"I worked in Toledo and Cleveland. I'll tell you who it was for, if you have to know. But then I'd have to kill them too."

"How would they find out you told me?"

"The same way you found out I made a call. We've been married a year, but I was with the organization more than twenty. They'd know. And even if they didn't, I couldn't take that chance."

She stretched a hand across the table. He covered it with one of his. "I'm sorry about before," she said. "Just when I start thinking we're a normal married couple, something comes up to remind me."

"What's normal?"

The waitress brought their meals. They ate mostly in silence, breaking it with innocuous comments on the tin advertising signs and old bric-a-brac decorating the walls. Finally she pushed away her plate. "I'm stuffed."

"No dessert?"

"Are you kidding? You never eat dessert."

"Another cup of coffee."

Her expression flattened. "You're waiting for someone."

"Don't worry, you won't see him."

They asked for a refill. When their cups were empty, Laurie went to the women's room while Macklin paid the bill. When they left the building, they found a fold of blue paper tucked under one of their windshield wipers. Macklin read what was written on it, then tore it into tiny pieces and let them flutter.

"A name?" Laurie asked.

"An address." He opened the door on the passenger's side and held it for her.

Wild Bill was napping in his chair on the back deck when his telephone rang. He went inside and picked up the receiver just before the machine kicked in. He listened, then said, "What changed your mind?"

"My horoscope," Grinnell's voice said. "What time Saturday?"

"They close at nine. Just before then."

The receiver clicked. Wild Bill worked the plunger, then pecked out a number.

" 'Sup?" asked Mark Twain, when he recognized the voice.

Wild Bill said shit under his breath. Mark only talked like a Budweiser commercial when he was on parrot tranquilizers. "Can you talk?"

"Sure. I just can't walk." He giggled.

"Man, I need you lucid."

There was a rustle on the other end; Mark sitting up, running his fingers through his dreads. "Okay, what?"

They made arrangements in a series of one-word sentences only they understood. When Wild Bill was sure Mark was sober enough not to forget them five minutes after they finished, he hung up, got the Beretta shotgun down from its perch atop one of the big timbers that held up the roof over the living room, broke it down, and coated every surface with graphite. When he put it back together and worked the pump, it slid as smoothly as foreskin.

FIFTEEN

Pamela Ziegenthaler answered the door with her hair tied up in a bandanna. She wore a buffalo plaid shirt with the sleeves rolled up past her forearms and the tail hanging out over stretch jeans. Her bare feet were stuck in woven sandals. Macklin thought of *I Love Lucy*.

"I got your message," she greeted. "I didn't expect you to come by. I'm getting some cleaning done; no telling when I'll get another chance until after the autograph party."

"I'm sorry, Mother. We'll come back later."

Macklin spoke up quickly. "I've got some business in Bowling Green. I thought Laurie's time would be better spent with you."

They'd argued about the decision, but he'd convinced her there was more risk involved with two. That hadn't made all her anger go away. She suspected there was more to it, and she was right.

"Well, I'll put you to work. I need someone to help me move the refrigerator so I can scrub behind it."

Laurie said, "I thought you had a woman come in."

"I let her go. She was a snoop. I didn't see any point in paying someone to gossip about me to her other employers."

Macklin wondered what part Grinnell had played in that decision.

"I don't do windows," Laurie said.

"I didn't ask you to, dear. I've seen how you clean. It's your young muscles I'm after. Business, you said?" she asked Macklin. "You said you were retired."

"I have investments. Mostly they look after themselves, but every now and then."

"Is that what you wanted to talk to me about?"

He said, "I'll be back in a couple of hours. I'll take you both out to dinner."

"I'll accept that offer. Benjamin called. He's stuck in Toledo for the next couple of days. You'd think he was the only man on the company payroll."

The address Macklin had found on his windshield belonged to a store that sold musical instruments near the Bowling Green University campus. Drum sets dressed the display windows and a candy-apple-red Stratocaster with a fifty-thousand-dollar price tag leaned aristocratically inside a glass case on a stand. A high ledge behind the counter supported glistening violins, gold snares, and amplifiers; trombones, trumpets, and saxophones hung from pegs on the wall below it. Keyboards and microphone stands competed for floor space with racks of picks, strings, reeds, and sheets of music. A poster tacked to the counter announced the appearance locally of a traditional Irish band.

Macklin waited while a gangly customer of about twenty paid for his purchase, a set of earphones and a twelve-volt battery. The young man's head was shaved and he had arrows tattooed on the back of his scalp, labeled YES and NO, like the rear of a semi-truck trailer. He walked out, carrying his sack and dragging the cuffs of his baggy pants.

"Sir?"

The counterman looked like an ex-professional wrestler, thin bleached hair to his shoulders, brown Fu Manchu moustache drooling from the corners of his wide mouth. Biceps and belly strained the material of a T-shirt advertising the four-century European tour of the Black Plague.

"Phil Lavery told me about your shop," Macklin said.

"Sorry, don't know him."

"He said you might say that. He said it might help if I mentioned Wapakoneta."

The counterman nodded. His face was glum. He moved to the far end of the counter, swung up a hinged flap, and came out from behind it. He was severely bowlegged — years of deep knee-bends with barbells resting across his shoulders — and the shortened tendons in his arms prevented them from hanging straight. He twisted the latch on the front door and turned the sign around in the window so that the CLOSED side faced out. "In back."

Macklin followed him behind the counter and through a fire door marked AUTHORIZED PERSONNEL ONLY into a combination workshop and storage area lit only by an overhead bulb and during the day a skylight with a heavy grid protecting the glass. Crates and boxes were stacked nearly to the rafters and tools hung on a pegboard above a workbench and littered its chipboard surface. Industrial-size padded clamps held a bass viol in place on the bench; the instrument was in the process of being restrung. A coil of string that looked like piano wire hung on a corner of the bench, waiting to be trimmed off.

The wrestler selected a key from a ring attached by a retractable cord to a metal case on his belt, unlocked a drawer shaped like a bin under the bench, removed an assortment of tuning hammers and needle-nose pliers, dumped them on the bench, and pulled up a false bottom. Eight handguns lay on a chamois cloth in the exposed compartment, their butts and barrels reversed so that they fit together like chicken drumsticks in a supermarket package.

"I don't deal full auto," the wrestler said. "That's a year and a day in this state, no plea bargain. I don't have room for long guns, shotguns and rifles. These days I make more off woodwinds. Every parent in Bowling Green thinks his kid's a virtuoso."

Macklin was only half listening. He ignored the Glocks and Berettas and picked up a Dan Wesson .38 Special revolver with a four-inch barrel. The chambers were empty.

"That comes with interchangeable barrels: eight, six, two and a half. I can let you have the works for six hundred."

"How much without the extra barrels?"

"Still six. Can't sell barrels without the revolver. I tried."

He aimed at a packing crate across the

room, dry-fired the Wesson. "Trigger pull's stiff."

"That's on account of it's new. It'll loosen up with practice. I don't sell used pieces. That one came in a batch that fell off the back of a truck."

"How long did you have to follow it before that happened?"

"See, that's the point. A man's time is worth something, even in this economy."

"Is it on a hot list?"

"The guys that owned the truck don't report losses. It's clean."

"What about cartridges?"

The wrestler produced another key and unlocked a bin-drawer next to the one he'd opened. "You know about Wapakoneta?"

"No."

"No, I don't guess Phil'd tell you. This fellow Anderson came short ten or fifteen grand on a loan. The guy Toledo sent to his house got hot and squiffed him. The wife walked in on it, so he squiffed her too. Fixed it up to look like murder-suicide. Toledo came down and sprayed some cash around to make sure it stuck. I provided the ordnance. It's the dirtiest deal I ever was in on. They like to use it whenever I talk about quitting. You know: 'You're in this far, and the cops in Wapakoneta never did trace the gun, but that don't mean someone won't make an anonymous phone call.' " He scooped a short-barreled .44 out of the drawer and pointed it at Macklin. "This one's loaded."

Macklin didn't move. The wrestler gestured with the barrel toward the ceiling. Macklin lifted his hands then. He was still holding the empty .38 in his right.

"I've never been to Wapakoneta," he said.

"What's the difference? I'm holding you for the cops. If you know Phil Lavery, they'll want to know you. Maybe they'll go easier on me for the other. I'm done walking around with it." He reached behind his back and drew a cellular telephone out of his hip pocket. He glanced at it one instant to dial 911 with his thumb.

Macklin swept his right hand down, cracking the .38's barrel across the wrestler's wrist. The wrestler yelped and the .44 thudded the floor. Macklin scooped up the coil of violin wire with his left hand, looped a length around the wrestler's thick neck, spun him around, and drew back on the wire. The wrestler dropped his telephone and clawed at his neck, the veins on his biceps standing out like rope. He raised one foot and kicked, fighting for leverage.

His foot went through the belly of the bass viol clamped to the bench. The instrument came away with the foot and flew apart when he stamped the floor. His fingers pried at the wire, but it was sunk almost out of sight. He heaved backward. Macklin, back-pedaling with him, toppled a stack of crates, stumbled, and struck the wall hard, pinned between it and the wrestler's bulk.

The man was as strong as a bull, and Macklin was out of practice. He hitched the wire twice around the revolver's barrel and twisted, drawing it tighter than he could through muscle power alone. The wrestler made cooking noises in his throat. He managed to plant one heel against the wall, shoved away, ducked his head, and tried to throw Macklin forward over his back; but his strength was waning. One of his knees buckled. Macklin spread his feet for leverage and leaned back. The wrestler snapped his leg straight through sheer will and threw his weight to the side. Macklin barked his ribs against the bench. Tools jangled on the peg-board, a rubber mallet fell off its hook and glanced off his shoulder. He gave the revolver another half twist. Bracing himself against the bench he jerked the wrestler upright and turned, swiveling him off his heels and increasing the torque. Something crunched underfoot; the wrestler's cell phone.

A stubby hand shot out toward the tools scattered on the bench and found a pair of needle-nose pliers that came to a wicked point, but Macklin pulled him away and the handle slid out of his grip. Air whistled through the wrestler's nostrils in a high-pitched sob.

His weight began to sag. Macklin resisted at first, sensing a trick, but a disk shifted in his back and he followed the man down, maintaining pressure. The wrestler fell to his knees, then toppled forward onto his face. Macklin knelt astride him and tried to twist the gun again, but it wouldn't budge. The wrestler's limbs began to twitch.

Macklin didn't let up for a full minute after the twitching stopped. Then he extricated the gun and groped at the man's lacerated neck for a pulse.

Finding none, he sat back on his heels, hung his head, and filled and emptied his lungs ten times. He was shaking — from muscular spasm, not fear — and his wind came out in shudders. He drew a sleeve across his streaming forehead. Garroting was a young man's game.

Something rattled and banged. Someone was trying the locked front door. He stood, staggered a little, and found his balance. His side ached. He had a kink in his back and his left arm tingled below the spot where the falling mallet had struck a nerve.

The drawer the wrestler had drawn the .44 from contained a box of cartridges for the Dan Wesson .38 Special and a Ziploc bag with the three interchangeable barrels inside. He might have bent the one he had subduing the damn ape. He unscrewed it, screwed the two-and-a-half-inch into its place, and put the bag in a pocket, along with the barrel he'd removed. He loaded the revolver and stuck the box in another pocket.

Whoever had tried the door had either given up or gone for help.

Macklin looked around. He hadn't touched anything that would preserve prints, and the curious party outside had smeared any he might have left on the door handle when he'd entered the shop. He pulled his shirt cuff down over his palm, found the bolt to the back door, and let himself out into the alley behind the building. It was empty in the light of a street lamp at the end except for a Dumpster and what remained of a dead raccoon after it had been run over by a succession of sanitation trucks. He threaded the revolver under his belt and dropped his shirttail over the butt.

Blank walls faced him on both sides, but he slumped his shoulders as he walked away, taking several inches off his height to discourage accurate description. You never knew who might be watching in a college town.

SIXTEEN

The interview room smelled of pencils, that resonant mix of cedar and graphite that always reminded him of grammar school. The table was steel with a laminate top and bolted to the floor. The wires attached to the switch on the interviewer's side would go down inside the legs and connect to the intercom outside the one-way mirror that hadn't fooled anyone since *The Defenders*. Light came in through a panel in the ceiling made of fluted shatterproof glass. There were dents in the beige-painted drywall just large enough to have been left by the heads of reluctant interviewees, if not by a mallet in the hands of a watch commander with an undergraduate degree in psychology. Not an unpleasant room, for all that, and certainly no more depressing than a hospital emergency waiting room with its professionally tended plants and collection of uninteresting magazines.

Grinnell was a connoisseur of both places. At age three he'd waited with his mother and brother at Queensway General for the news about his father, and he'd spent a total of three days in these identical surroundings at the time of his arrest for conspiracy to violate the laws of interstate commerce. His mother had been in and out of treatment for various complaints real and imagined; he had played the dutiful son until he was old enough to operate a motor vehicle and drive away.

He'd been in this one almost four hours. There was no clock, but he had his watch and he was a good judge of time without having to look at it every few minutes. An officer in uniform — not one of the pair who had come to his condominium — had escorted him to the men's room down the hall an hour and a half earlier, but apart from that his stay had been uninterrupted by human contact. The officer had gone in with him and waited while he used the urinal. There had been no window in the rest room, no other exit except the door they'd entered through, but the man had taken no chances. That told him — if he hadn't already guessed — that he was being detained for something or someone important. He knew for what and probably for whom, but whenever his thoughts drifted that direction he changed their course. Policemen were no more telepathic than anyone else, but a man could trap himself by assuming.

Grinnell had been home an hour when the knock had come to his door. He'd had time meanwhile to change out of his redneck camouflage and stash the Browning BDA he'd bought from Sunny Wong.

His condo occupied two floors of a historic row house overlooking Toledo and Maumee Bay. Shortly after moving in, he'd found a shaft hidden behind a panel near the kitchen ceiling, a remnant of the Victorian mania for ventilation, and that discovery had erased the last trace of unease about his long financial commitment. He'd suspected he'd find use for it one day.

That day had been long in coming, but upon returning from greater Cincinnati and before changing his clothes he'd climbed a stepladder, crawled inside the shaft, pried loose another panel, and deposited the pistol behind a joist belonging to the row house on the other side of the common wall.

That was the best part. The cache wouldn't withstand a really thorough police search, but those were rare, and even then the evidence wouldn't be allowed in court without a search warrant issued to his neighbor's address. In the unlikely event of a friendly ruling, the forbidden item was evidence of only a misdemeanor. There was nothing to connect it with Hilliard or Sunny or the Vulpo crime family. He'd driven it from his mind immediately after replacing the panels.

He was getting hungry, but the greasy corn chips and Twinkies he'd seen in the machine outside the room held no appeal. He was eating healthy these days, partly under Pamela's influence, partly because of his awareness of middle age. Fish, skinless chicken, vegetables lightly steamed. He was getting to be as ordinary as he pretended.

He wasn't under arrest, and so technically was not entitled to ask to use the telephone. Technically he was free to go, but he knew he'd be arrested if he tried to leave. That would force him to call an attorney and bring the Vulpos into it. He preferred to wait things out, just as the police preferred to let him. Four hours was more than time enough for whomever they were expecting to arrive from any place he might be expected to start from; the rest was to make Grinnell doubt himself. In most cases it probably worked.

He occupied his time with a childhood game, silently reciting the titles of Shakespeare's plays in the order of authorship.

The Comedy of Errors. Love's Labour's Lost. Henry VI, parts I, II, and III . . .

In his early life, he'd been considered something of a prodigy. He'd learned to read at two and a half, and at five entertained houseguests by performing the first act of *Lady Windermere's Fan* from memory, much to the amazement and alarm of his mother, who'd believed that precocious genius led to a nervous breakdown in one's teens, followed by a lifetime of drooling idiocy and familial dependence. In any case the experience of his father had soured her on intellectual achievement, and to save him from his heritage she'd enrolled him in those pursuits she thought more suited to normal adolescence: soccer (which she insisted upon calling "football"), friendship with the dullard offspring of neighbors who attended American movies and thought dinner theater the apex of culture, and a social calendar chockablock with cheerleaders and girls who read magazines with teen idols on the covers. Close observation of their behavior had taught him how to cloak himself in bland disguise.

Romeo and Juliet. Richard II. A Midsummer Night's Dream. King John . . .

His flight from home, therefore, had been a rebellion against both parents. He'd dredged canals, made change behind counters, shoplifted electronic equipment for quick cash. But steering a course opposite both high- and middlebrow required constant vigilance, and in time he'd succumbed to the tastes of his paternity. He would not finish his formal education, because that would have pleased the old rake whose name he'd shared, but the knowledge that if he had done so he'd be eminently qualified to join the faculty of a respectable university, and had chosen instead to squander his gifts in the underworld, satisfied him down to the heels. He'd whiled away many an hour watching the entrances of credit unions whose safes his companions were cracking, chronicling the works of the Bard from memory.

Julius Caesar. As You Like It. Twelfth Night. Hamlet . . .

At times, he recognized, his ability to detach himself from his thoughts had caused problems. He hadn't been concentrating in Hilliard. The risk factor in video stores was so low, and case work so routine, that he'd merely gone through the motions: seeing and noting, but not looking beyond the superficial. Assuming. It had cost a man his life, Wild Bill's crew its low profile, and Grinnell his reputation for reliability. Before Hilliard, Tommy Vulpo had taken him for granted, not altogether a bad thing. What had happened there had attracted Toledo's notice. Grinnell's plan to coast under the radar into comfortable early retirement was jeopardized, his hostel in Myrtle in danger of exposure; and he caught himself thinking, and returned to his recitation.

All's Well That Ends Well. Othello. King Lear. Measure for Measure . . .

The door opened and in came Edgar Prine, commander of the Ohio State Police Armed Robbery Task Force.

Macbeth.

He was more formidable in person than on television; what media analysts called a "hot personality," impressive when encountered on the stage of a church hall or a tent meeting, pounded flat by harsh lights and the two dimensions of the camera. His physical presence filled a room that had been small to begin with, and his expanse of black suit threatened to suck Grinnell into it like a black hole. Grinnell resisted without great effort. His own studied effect was like eiderdown, which danced and floated and lacked the mass to surrender to the pull of gravity.

Prine wore a professional smile, teeth clamped together like pliers. He was carrying a green leather folder with the Ohio State seal embossed on it in gold. It was the next best thing to swaddling himself in the state flag; but it wasn't wise to belittle the man, even to oneself. He hadn't risen to his current position and held it so long against the hurricane force of politics by being the pompous ass he appeared. It might even have been an artfully constructed facade, like Grinnell's own.

In fact he was sure of it. The hazard in living a role was to presume that everyone else was genuine.

Close on Prine's heels came a smaller man who could have lost himself in his own shadow, let alone his companion's. He was fifty and could have passed for older, round-shouldered in a suit that was not quite a suit, the coat a shade darker than the trousers, but equally past hope of pressing. His grizzled hair was amateurishly cut and he carried his chin at an upward tilt that in anyone else might have been mistaken for arrogance. Grinnell suspected he was severely shortsighted and had either left his reading glasses behind or was in denial about needing them. All this was perhaps less the result of artifice, but on the whole here was another example of a creature who was greater than the sum of its parts. These were deep waters.

He recognized the man in a muzzy sort of way from public appearances with Prine, and more specifically from behind the wheel of an official automobile powering up Tommy Vulpo's driveway as Grinnell was driving down. He understood then the process that had led all three men from there to here. Chance was a treacherous mistress, filthy and unpredictable.

This too he banished from memory. His best chance of leaving the building unescorted was not only to present a clean slate, but to be one as well.

Captain Edgar Prine sat down at the interview table, laid his folder on its top, and stretched his arm across to envelop the hand of the man seated across from him. He introduced himself and Farrell McCormick, who remained standing and made no move to shake hands. Then Prine built some business out of spreading open the folder and looking at the top sheet, as if he'd forgotten what it contained.

"You're John Grinnell Benjamin?"

The man shook his head. "I'm Benjamin Grinnell. I changed it when I applied for citizenship. That's the form you have in front of you."

"Why'd you change it?"

"I never liked it much. I've never considered myself the John type."

"What type is that?"

"A regular sort of fellow who throws Super Bowl parties."

"That's right, you're Canadian by birth. I guess hockey's your game."

"Not particularly."

"So much for sports. You don't look like a Ben, either, if you don't mind my saying so. Why'd you keep Grinnell?"

"It was a family name on my mother's side. She was a cousin of George Bird Grinnell."

Prine smiled ignorance.

"He wrote a history of the Cheyenne Indians, among other things. It's still taught in anthropology courses, nearly eighty years after it was published."

"I guess you're proud of that. Well, why not? Eighty years. That's quite a thing."

Grinnell said nothing.

"Do you know why you were asked to come here today?"

"The officers said they wanted to ask some questions."

"That isn't really an answer."

Grinnell said nothing.

Prine peeled aside the photostat copy of Grinnell's citizenship application. It had been stamped APPROVED. The next sheet was a report of his arrest for smuggling cigarettes. No stamp there. "You smoke?"

Grinnell shook his head.

"Says here you were apprehended in Michigan on an outstanding warrant for trying to sell sixty cartons of Marlboros to a supermarket in Sandusky. I guess you're like those old-time bootleggers who never took a nip themselves. Professional pride."

Grinnell was silent.

McCormick spoke up. "You know that money's used to support terrorists. You a terrorist, Benjamin?"

"Grinnell."

Prine smiled his grit-toothed smile. "I'm sure the lieutenant was just calling you by your first name. We're pretty informal around here, Ben. You can call me Ed, and the lieutenant prefers Mac. No one's called him Farrell since his mother passed over. That's right, isn't it, Mac?"

"My wife still calls me it sometimes, when she's mad."

"Try living with Edgar. What's yours call you, Ben? You married?"

"No."

"Divorced?"

"No."

"Well, that's as far as I can follow that line. Don't ask, don't tell, you know?"

No response; not even irritation at the implication he was gay. He might have been at that. There was a blurred delicacy about the man's features that reminded him of an old movie actor. Not a matinee idol, but the best friend of the hero in a B feature. There was nothing insolent about Grinnell's silence, no hint of defiance, just a polite expression of waiting for a question he could answer and help out the interviewer. That was an acquired skill, and for the first time the captain was less than confident of a positive end to the conversation.

"What do you do, Ben?" he asked.

"I'm a facilitator with American Dreams Home Supplies. I help maintain consistency of service throughout the chain."

"That's a Toledo company, isn't it?"

"Yes, the headquarters is downtown."

"You know it's mobbed up?"

"Mobbed up?"

"It's one of a dozen companies Joe

Vulpo has big investments in. You know Joe?"

"I've heard of him."

"Tommy's his son. You know Tommy?"

"I've heard of him as well."

"You went to see him three days ago."

Grinnell watched him with curiosity on his face.

"I know you saw us," Prine said. "Details are important in your work."

"They are."

"Maybe you just needed a place to turn around, and there was Tommy's driveway. But you can see the coincidence. Then there's your record."

Nothing. Prine turned over the old arrest report and looked at a note scribbled on a memo sheet.

"Travel a lot?" he asked.

"Quite a bit."

"Pretty hard on a car, even a Lexus. Miamitown officer spotted your car parked in front of a dry cleaner's there. I put some men on it, but you never showed. I asked Toledo P.D. to send someone to your place here. You want to tell us why you left your car clear down by Cincinnati?"

Grinnell scratched his cheek and refolded his hands on the table.

"Maybe it broke down. All that wear and

tear. You're not the hitchhiking type, so I'm guessing you rented a car and drove it back here. The Lexus was still there a little while ago. I checked. Guess the place you called hasn't gotten around to it yet."

Nothing. Prine sat back. McCormick looked down at Grinnell with the sad bored face of an experienced mortician.

"I don't know why we're wasting this kind of time on you," he said. "You're a U.S. citizen because a mob lawyer dealt you out of a felony conviction, but you're basically a penny player. Seven years later and you're still out hustling. You're no prize, Benjamin."

"We all make allowances for the lieutenant," Prine said. "He's borderline Tourette's. He hasn't reached the stage where you curse in public and make rude noises. He's just blunt."

McCormick wore away. "Tommy has to be thinking the same thing. You were an okay front man, so he gave you a little more to do, put you to work casing video stores, but it was too much. You tripped over your own elbow, got a man killed, and now you're on the burner. I'm thinking that's why you slunk out of his place carrying your balls in a paper bag.

What do you figure he'll do when he sees your face on TV?"

"May I have a glass of water?"

McCormick looked sadder. "Another day or so and you can have all of Maumee Bay."

Prine said, "Don't overdo it, Mac. You feel faint, Ben? Dehydration sneaks up on you."

"No, just a little thirsty."

"Okay if it's from the tap? I don't know if they have bottled here."

"From the tap is fine."

The captain closed the green folder and stood. "It's hot in here with three people. Departmental cutbacks; they seal off these rooms from the central air to save energy. Bad for the blood pressure. We'll leave you alone for a few minutes. I'll send in water."

"Thank you, Captain."

Outside the room, the two detectives switched roles. McCormick's face lifted, and Prine's was grim.

"Smooth character," the lieutenant said. "He doesn't scare, and he won't use a story even when you make one up for him."

"A crook with company manners is still a crook."

"Kick him?"

Prine drummed his fingers on the edge of the folder. "Yeah. If we blow him now, Tommy'll stay away from him like AIDS. That puts us back in the dugout." He thumped McCormick's chest with a corner of the folder. "Closed tail. If he spots us he'll just lead us to every American Dreams store in the Cuyahoga Valley."

"I didn't know American Dreams was Vulpo."

"It isn't. He wouldn't be working there if it was. You can't bluff a bluffer, but that doesn't mean you can't try."

"If I was Tommy, I'd have sent him to the showers after Hilliard."

"If you were Tommy, Grinnell would've left Northwood in the cargo compartment of that Lexus." He paused. "You were scary in there."

"You think? Going in, I thought I'd throw a chair or something, pound the table. I couldn't find the motivation."

"Save it," Prine said. "We're going to wind this one up in Kevlar."

SEVENTEEN

"Fucking gingerbread village," Carlos said. "I lived here, I'd run down the fucking mayor to get out."

Mark said, "Not me. I'd open up a cockshop. All these horny old guys married to old bats selling potpourri, them rickety benches with the heart-shaped holes, they got to drive all the way into Toledo for pussy." He'd never sounded so black.

"Pipe down or roll the windows up," Wild Bill said mildly. He was enjoying the scenery in an ironic way, two rows of 150-year-old brick buildings painted country blue with fake white columns plastered to the fronts. Six gift shops, a place that did fancy nails, and no place to buy a screw-driver. Strip malls were a crime against Main Street.

Donny drove twenty-three miles an hour and said nothing. They were using his personal car, a battered Chevelle worn down to primer all around with a 380 Coup deVille engine grumbling under the sun-powdered hood. Wild Bill insisted they all attend trial runs, mainly to give Carlos a chance to bust their balls with "better" escape routes and get them out of his system. Donny wasn't easily distracted, but Wild Bill was always keyed up after the real deal, and with a shotgun across his lap it would be just too tempting. He'd be one happy cowboy when the bookstore was behind them and the partnership dissolved.

There would be no getaway through downtown. The council had reconfigured the street into a zigzag by planting trees and flower beds, discouraging speeders; he could see them racing through at seventy, sparks showering off the frame and pieces of suspension trailing the pavement. No reason to have to point that out to Donny.

The residential neighborhoods were potluck: wedding-cake Victorians, 1960s ranch styles, modulars dating back no further than pet rocks. They passed two baby-boom schools with trailer-type temporary classrooms dropped in to handle the new housing tracts, three sparkling bank branches with non-geo-specific names, combo gas stations and convenience stores, a warehouse outlet that might as well have been called Some Assembly Required. Squat-and-gobble fast-food joints,

Wal-Mart Supercenter, Discount Tire, Chevy and Honda dealerships, and not a stick in them older than the transmission Donny had rebuilt from junkyard scrap. A brick shell was going up on a dirt lot with a hangar door–size sign out front announcing the site of a new Panera Bread. Farther out on the plain smoothed by the mighty Ohio River, Wild Bill could see the first of the subdivisions bordering on one another like European countries, to half-million-dollar houses with Palladian windows and four-car garages, still smelling of fresh sawdust and curing concrete; they stood among artificial hills built from landfill and carpeted with blue-green sod. He might have been in any town in North America, regardless of size or the source of its economy.

They slowed down for a construction crew grading for two additional lanes and turned at last into a parking lot with a Hallmark, a pharmacy that sold package liquor, a health club, a video outlet — twinge of nostalgia there, but life went on — and a bookstore with a sheet of glass for a front wall and remainders stacked on long folding tables under the overhang. Customers loitered there and passed in and out through glass double doors.

They'd deliberately chosen the hour past

dinner Saturday for the reconnoiter, when the streets were paved with entertainment-hungry motorists and the average wait to get through a traffic light involved two changes. It would be quieter later in the evening, when next week's thing went down, but to know a route when all the obstacles were in place was to know it thoroughly, like a woman without her first-date manners. There were no regular spaces available near the businesses. Donny pulled into a vacant one with a sign saying it was reserved for expectant mothers (Carlos wondered if there was a slot for customers with clap) and switched off the engine. They sat there for a while watching the customer flow.

Wild Bill said, "You wonder who's home watching *Survivor.*"

"Skin magazines and the out-of-town papers," Carlos said. "That's the profit margin. These places'd go under if all they had was Isabel Allende."

Mark Twain grunted. Wild Bill suspected he was coming down from the parrot pills, when his mood was ugliest. "What you know about Isabel Allende? All the comic books out of circ in the Jackson library?"

"Hey, I read. Not much else to do when Paulie D'Onofrio's got his buttons out looking for you."

"I keep forgetting you rode along on the St. Valentine's Day Massacre."

"Man, I know you're shitting, but down in Little Mexico, that one wouldn't even make the papers. That's how come Tommy Vulpo does his recruiting in the Spanish neighborhoods."

Wild Bill wondered if Carlos even spoke the language. The wetbacks in El Paso would've broken him like a piñata. He said, "I'm going in, look around."

"What for?" Mark asked. "That's Grinnell's end."

"First he's in, then he's out, then he's back in. Who knows where he'll be in a week?"

"Pussy." Carlos spat his *p*'s, sprinkling the back of Wild Bill's neck. "That last fuckup brought out the yellow."

Mark said, "It's a bookstore. What's to see?"

"There's always a back room, where they do the ordering and keep the extra stock. Maybe they don't lock the back door. Is there a public toilet? How many doors we got to watch? Shit like that."

"Send in Donny. No one sees him anyway. He looks like a guy you see hanging around Science Fiction." Mark was sullen.

The driver turned his scruffy-bearded face on Wild Bill. Panic shone in his eyes. He never showed it when the road was all he had to face.

"There's a crowd. No one'll notice me." Wild Bill opened the door.

Carlos said, "See if they got *Latin Labia*."

Wild Bill looked at the man in the backseat: tightly curled hair low on the forehead, bunched, angry features, thick Pancho Villa moustache. He looked like an old Frito ad.

"Anything else? You want me to pull out my cock so they'll remember me?"

"I didn't say get it. I said see if they got it. I might pick it up next Saturday."

"After next Saturday you can hire Ricky Martin's asshole and bugger it all day Sunday." He got out and thunked the door shut.

An eleven-by-fourteen placard in the window advertised the Francis Spain signing. There was a color mock-up of the new book, *Serpent in Eden*, a blown-up quote, "Awesome!" from MTV, and a smug picture of the author leaning against a red barn wall with his arms crossed in a sweatshirt and khakis. He brushed his teeth but apparently not his hair and he had one of those tans you sprayed on. Copies of the book were stacked next to the sign, with one propped face out on top, and there was a cardboard display box on the other side holding up rows of last year's *Love Song* in glistening paperback.

Wild Bill held the door for a fat woman carrying two full plastic bags. She didn't say thanks or fuck you or kiss my ass. He missed the courtly manners of the far West.

People were lined up at the checkout with their selections under their arms. Others prowled the aisles between the racks, browsed among the magazines and discounted art and travel books on the remainder table, blocking the paths of employees pushing carts with more books to shelve. There was no coffee shop, no public rest room for either sex. Two cashiers worked the counter. No in-your-face security, and nobody sticking out like Andy Sipowitz among the looky-loos.

Wild Bill wandered toward the children's section in back. A door marked EMPLOYEES ONLY stood propped open with a stack of books with torn jackets. He glimpsed more books piled on metal utility shelves, an open door to an employee rest room, a plywood counter holding up a computer monitor hemmed in by bales of paper, no employees in his line of sight.

He took down a picture book with glazed cardboard covers and pictures of all kinds of big trucks: the young father looking for something for his toddler son. He had on a blue work shirt over a gray T-shirt and jeans. He might be working at any of the plants he'd seen on the other side of town. Not that it mattered. The customers dressed every way possible, not counting evening wear and barefoot in overalls. That stiff Grinnell put too much thought into trying to blend in. Wild Bill wondered why he'd changed his mind about backing out. Maybe that crack Wild Bill had made about Myrtle hadn't been such a shot in the dark after all. There was something not quite right about the way Grinnell presented himself, went out of his way to be invisible even among his accomplices. Wild Bill knew the difference between a tame cougar and a domestic cat. He put back the truck book and looked at three shelves of Dr. Seuss. The man must have been an insomniac.

He was flipping through *Horton Hears a Who*, his head swimming with rhymes, when a heavy door slammed shut in the back room and three people came out into the store, a short-haired middle-aged woman in a blazer pinning a name tag to one lapel followed by a man close to her in age, and a younger woman, a pretty blonde in a silk blouse and tailored slacks with a high rise that showed off her narrow waist. She was *Playboy* material: not quite busty enough for the centerfold, but worth a spread in *The Girls of the Big Ten*, lithe, well-scrubbed, and golden. She dressed a little too well for a college student, but no ticket clerk would demand to see her student ID. She was too young for the man, but he sensed they were together.

"This won't take a minute," the older woman told the couple. "Look around all you want. If you see anything you like, you can use my discount." She strode off from them toward the front counter.

Wild Bill watched the couple over the brightly illustrated pages in front of him, curious about their relationship with a store worker — the manager, he guessed, by her age and don't-fuck-with-me walk. There was nothing to the man. Medium height, medium weight, medium everything; thinning temples, tired face set in a patient mask. You saw the most faded men with the best-looking women, and this one had been left forgotten on somebody's dashboard a long time. Wild Bill wouldn't have looked at him twice in any place but a place he was getting ready to rob.

These things Wild Bill thought, then realized how long he'd been thinking them, and how much of the time he'd spent watching the man and not the woman. He was in his middle forties, fit-enough looking for his age but no Bruce Willis. That kind could surprise you in the mountains, climbing all day shouldering heavy packs and rifles, outdistancing the young sprinters and lifters who'd loped out in front at dawn. And this one seemed to be paying more attention to his surroundings than the stock. Wandering a little away from the woman, who had stopped in Home Decorating, he read the spines in Photography, took one down, glanced inside, and put it back; but all the time he kept track of the traffic through the doors, the people coming his way up the aisle, the cashier behind the counter talking with the woman in the blazer.

He might have been casing the place himself.

Cop, Wild Bill thought. Advance security, checking things out for the Francis Spain tour. He reminded Wild Bill a little of

Grinnell. Their side didn't have the monopoly.

The manager came striding back. The pretty blonde returned a book on country homes to the shelf and joined the pair in Photography. Wild Bill put back Dr. Seuss and drifted that way.

"Nothing?" said the manager. Wild Bill couldn't read her name tag and he didn't want to be caught trying.

The young woman said, "I can't concentrate. I'm famished after all that cleaning."

Facing each other in profile, they bore a close resemblance. He guessed mother and daughter.

"Well, let's eat. Where are you taking us?"

"You choose," said the man. "I'm a stranger here, and Laurie keeps talking about places that aren't there anymore."

"Careful, dear," the mother said. "That's how you date yourself. How about the Bread Basket? It's not far, and they make the best carrot cake in town."

They drifted out the back. Wild Bill didn't follow.

He was relieved to know the man's connection was personal, not professional, but he was glad he'd come in when he had. If the man was there next Saturday night, he'd be someone to watch. Wild Bill had learned his lesson about civilian heroes.

He scooped a box off the Audio Books rack — the cover was a smaller version of the *Serpent in Eden* jacket, with a picture of Matt Damon, the reader, next to Spain's on the back — waited his turn in line, and slapped it on the counter. The woman cashier he'd seen talking with the manager charged him thirty bucks and change.

He slid two twenties across the counter. "Boss check up on you every night?"

She looked at him briefly, then shook open a plastic bag. She was a redhead with freckles the size of poker chips. He could tell she approved of what she saw. Not every woman went for that rangy gunfighter look, but when they went, they went clean over the fence. Her tag said her name was Marjorie.

"No, she's just nervous about next week. She wants to make sure we ordered enough books." She showed him a flyer announcing the Spain event and stuffed it into the bag with the audiobook. She gave him his change.

"Guy on the tape? Looks like you got enough for everybody in town."

"They come in from all over. Last week in Buffalo, New York, he signed a thousand copies in three hours. Buffalo's not much bigger than Myrtle."

"I don't think I could write my name that many times in three hours. He that good?"

"I loved his first. The new one just came in. You should get one for your wife and have him sign it. I don't know if he signs books on tape."

"I had a wife, I might. That her family she had with her?"

She was confused for a moment.

"Oh, Pamela? I didn't notice. If she has a family she never introduced them to any of us."

He underscored the name mentally.

"Treat you like mushrooms, I guess. Keep you in the dark and throw shit on you."

He could tell she'd heard that one, but she laughed anyway. It was like shining deer, not much sport.

"Maybe I'll drop by, meet the man. You working that night?" His fingers brushed hers as he accepted the bag.

Her freckles vanished into bright pink. "Whole staff's scheduled."

"Maybe I won't wait till Saturday."

He was almost out the door before he heard her say she could help the next person in line. Easy banks, slow trains, willing women. It was hard not to swagger.

EIGHTEEN

Prine, evidently determined to go on playing the good cop, had offered to return Grinnell to his apartment in an unmarked car. Grinnell, equally bent on playing the unadventurous acquiescent, had accepted. A plainclothesman who introduced himself as Detective Plenham chewed Trident and talked about the Indian motorcycle he was restoring throughout the first dozen blocks. Grinnell, normally attentive in tedious company — looking for tics to emulate — said nothing to encourage him. In time Plenham stopped droning and turned up the volume on the two-way radio. There was absolutely nothing happening in the city of Toledo to occupy the police.

In front of his building, Grinnell thanked the detective, got out, and walked up the front steps, careful not to look at any of the cars parked on the street. He knew he was being watched, knew also that Prine would have ordered them to be clever, and looking for them would only tip a cover the police already knew was just that, a cover. He'd been outed, but to abandon the masquerade now would be to admit defeat, and he had no practice at that.

In any case, he'd been Ben Grinnell so long he wouldn't know how to go back to being John Grinnell Benjamin. He barely remembered the fellow. A man had his choice of prisons, that was all. He could plead guilty and go to a six-by-eight cell or turn stool pigeon and go to North Dakota or put on his bars like a suit of clothes and wear them everywhere he went. A self-inflicted sentence was just as dismal as the other kind.

He rode the coffin-size elevator with its Edwardian cage and modern mechanism to his floor, grilled a cheese sandwich, and ate it with milk to fill the hole in his stomach. He tried listening to music, then turned off the stereo, giving it up as an artificial mood-altering device. He poured himself a glass of white wine, then poured it out after a few sips for the same reason. Finally he picked up the telephone and called Pamela's number in Myrtle. He didn't care if the wires were tapped. The police would find out about her sooner or later. That had been the reason for her in the first place. After next Saturday she would be useless to him — worse than useless; the link they would need to tie him to Wild Bill's crew and a felony murder charge for the video-store disaster. But until then he needed her more than ever.

Her machine kicked in on the fourth ring. He hung up without leaving a message and tried the bookstore. He'd given her a cellular telephone for her birthday, but she was always leaving it behind or neglecting to recharge it, and he'd forgotten the number from disuse. Pamela wasn't that careless except with things she didn't like. She was a passive-aggressive nightmare, like his mother, and after the young woman who answered at the bookstore put him on hold, he was a little surprised when it occurred to him he'd miss her. A little masochism seemed a small price to pay to avoid loneliness.

The young woman came back on. "I'm sorry, sir. She was here earlier, but she left."

"Did she say where she was going?"

"No — hang on." Someone was talking to her. "Okay, thanks. Sir? Someone heard her talking about going to the Bread Basket. That's —"

"I know what it is. Thanks." He broke the connection.

If that's where she was dining, she wasn't alone. It was one of the more expensive restaurants in Myrtle, and Pamela was extravagant only when someone else was paying. He was pretty sure who it would be, and it made him hesitate. But any company was preferable to his own that night. He scooped up the keys to the rental. He might catch them in time for dessert.

Macklin was actually relieved when Grinnell joined them in their booth.

Conversation with Pamela was a chore. When in a nod toward politeness she stopped chattering with Laurie about the autograph party and asked him if everything had gone well in Bowling Green, he'd fantasized telling her he'd had some trouble buying a gun and had been forced to strangle the seller to death, just to avoid that skeptical expression she wore even when he was telling her an innocuous truth. But he was pretty sure she'd have responded with the same look.

He forgave Laurie all her faults in the presence of her mother. Her childhood must have been as trying as his life with Donna. So far as he believed in forces outside the physical — he'd made so many corpses and hadn't seen a soul lifting away from any of them — he accepted Pamela as some kind of cosmic payback for his past behavior, but Laurie was an innocent victim.

Grinnell explained that his meetings had run shorter than expected, cleared up the mystery of how he'd found their party, and helped Pamela finish her enormous slice of carrot cake. Macklin ordered a second cup of coffee and Laurie calmed her nerves with a cordial. He'd felt her stiffen at his side when Grinnell appeared, had squeezed her hand beneath the table, providing support and warning at the same time. She'd responded by keeping her silence. Between Pamela's commentary on the elaborate preparations for Francis Spain's visit and Grinnell's holding forth about the inefficacy of business meetings in general, neither seemed to notice that Laurie wasn't contributing to the conversation.

It was an awkward situation, but probably no more so than some others taking place in the restaurant. Macklin, almost unconsciously maintaining his habit of paying attention to everything around him, could tell that the young couple gesticulating at a table for two in the corner was breaking up, and that the hilarity of the birthday celebration around the big round table in the center of the room was lost on the elderly guest of honor, a woman in a brocaded jacket faded on one sleeve from hanging unused in a room with unshaded windows; a young woman who might have been her granddaughter cut up her meat and fed it to her, taking part in the general chatter the whole time. Macklin felt a little less alien.

At length he paid the bill, over an argument from Grinnell, and the women adjourned to the rest room while the men waited in front of the restaurant for their cars. The sun had been down for hours.

"Beige SUV," Grinnell told the attendant, handing him his ticket.

Macklin asked him what had happened to his Lexus.

"It broke down in Cincinnati; computer problem, probably. I had it towed. I barely had time to rent this one and make the first meeting."

"I used to travel quite a bit. It's hard on the family life."

"Pamela's understanding. You were married before, weren't you?"

Macklin remembered the subject coming up in conversation with his mother-in-law. "Yes. I've got a son Laurie hasn't met yet."

"That complicates things."

"I think it's supposed to."

The tall square vehicle came around the corner of the building and squished to a stop in front of the door.

Macklin said, "You're Canadian, aren't you?"

Grinnell gave the attendant a dollar and turned to face Macklin. "I wasn't aware it showed."

"A little, the way you talk. I used to live close to Detroit. A lot of people come over from Windsor every day to work. You wouldn't know they were Canadian except for the way they pronounce some words."

" 'Oot and aboot'?" Grinnell exaggerated slightly.

"Those are two," Macklin said. "Your real name's John Benjamin, isn't it?"

Grinnell's expression didn't change. He nodded slightly, as if answering a question he'd asked himself. "I rearranged it a bit. You have that opportunity when you become a citizen. Pamela asked me to find out some things about you, too," he said.

"How's that working out?"

"Here come the ladies." Grinnell smiled past Macklin's shoulder. His voice dropped. "We should meet for a drink, you and I."

"When?"

"Later tonight. Not here. Everyone in Myrtle eavesdrops on everyone else. Do you know the Alehouse? It's on Route Sixty-five, on the river."

"I'll find it. Eleven o'clock."

"What's at eleven o'clock?" Pamela wound an arm around Grinnell's back. She'd had a split of chablis with her dinner and was a little tipsy.

"Boys' night out, dear," Grinnell said. "Peter and I are going to get to know each other better. You can spare me, can't you? I don't have to be back at work till Monday."

Laurie had taken Macklin's hand. She squeezed hard. He squeezed back. "I'll see he doesn't stay out too late," he told Pamela.

"Well, if I'm going to be without male companionship this evening, I'm commandeering your wife. You haven't checked into a hotel, have you?" She smiled at Laurie. Macklin squeezed her hand again.

"No, our bags are in the car. Are you sure you're up to having us? You've been all day cleaning."

"That's an argument in favor. A clean house is just wasted on Benjamin and me. If our men will promise not to wake up the neighborhood when they stagger in, they're welcome too."

Grinnell said, "I'll drive on ahead and get us a table. Toledo's a madhouse Saturday night."

"Toledo?" Pamela squinted up at him. "There are bars here in town."

"They close at midnight, darling. We'd just be warming up."

"You won't drink too much? The troopers are out for blood on weekends."

"We'll pace ourselves," Macklin said.

NINETEEN

Edgar Prine approved of morgues in general.

They appealed to his sense of order, with their isolated, well-lit autopsy rooms, their separate offices for the coroner, his deputies, and medical examiners, their viewing rooms with comfortable seating for visitors and closed-circuit monitors to spare those identifying friends and relatives the stench of formaldehyde and stale meat, and the rows of oversize file drawers containing their tagged and sheeted inventory. They kept the corpses alphabetical and off the streets.

He waited patiently, enjoying the climate-controlled atmosphere, while the attendant in the cold-room, a tidy Pakistani in a white lab coat that looked pressed, fiddled with the video camera until he had it in focus and pointed at the proper angle. Along the way Prine got glimpses of the attendant's face in extreme close-up and most of the corners of the room.

Prine shared the viewing room with a

Bowling Green police officer named Rosetta Alfiero, a stout young Hispanic with a pretty face and her black hair pinned up under her visored cap. As the first officer on the crime scene she had been assigned to escort the State Police captain. She was nervous, because of either Prine's rank and reputation or the surroundings or her temperament in general, and had chosen to stand rather than squirm in the seat next to his. She stood at his elbow, making impatient faces at the swinging images on-screen.

Finally they were looking at the bloated gray-blue face of a powerfully built male Caucasian in his mid to late thirties. His hair, damp from a recent body-scrubbing, was long, stringy, and colored an improbable shade of yellow. Purple bruises fingered out from an angry line around his neck where something thin had sliced through flesh and muscle. His eyes bulged and his tongue stuck out.

"Victim's name is Carroll Oster." Alfiero read from a spiral pad. "Carroll, that's with two *r*'s and two *l*'s."

"Like Carroll O'Connor."

The officer paused. Prine suspected she was too young to remember *All in the Family*.

"It came in as a citizen complaint," she went on. "Band student had a French horn on layaway, went to the shop to make the last payment and claim it. Oster promised it'd be there for practice this evening. When the kid found the place shut up, he figured Oster'd jumped to South America with his hundred and sixty-nine fifty. Nothing much was doing when he came in to the precinct house, so I went back there with him."

"What made you decide to go in?"

She looked at her notebook, as if the answer would be recorded there. She really was nervous. "Some of the local merchants leave their home numbers with us, in case there's a break-in and they have to come in and report what's missing, board up a window. I called his home number, got his sister. She said Carroll never closed up during business hours, brought in his lunch so he wouldn't miss making a sale. She worried about his health. He worked out too hard for a man coming up on middle age, didn't watch his diet. Prime stroke candidate. She authorized me to break down the door. I found him in the back room. Looked like he put up a fight; place was all torn up.

"Oster had a cache of handguns," she

continued. "We didn't find any papers. That's why we called Columbus. This didn't look like armed robbery, but if he was dealing weapons we figured the ARTF would want to know. You're more than we expected, Captain. We thought you'd send a trooper."

"Columbus radioed me on my way out of Toledo. I was there to talk to someone. When I hear murder and unregistered handguns in the same sentence, I follow up. Did Oster have a record?"

"Not for weapons. We busted a gambling ring five years ago. Some students were betting on college wrestling. He carried the slips. He rolled over on a local athletic booster and got nineteen hundred hours of community service. The booster went to Belize."

"Doesn't matter," Prine said. "He'd just be taking the fall for Toledo. Tommy Vulpo's got a piece of every office and campus pool this side of Kentucky. That makes this a professional killing."

"I disagree, Captain."

He swiveled to look up at her. She flushed.

"Not about Vulpo, Captain," she said. "What I mean, the killer used violin string he found on the premises. The end of it was still attached to what was left of a bass viol. Professionals usually bring their own weapons."

"You get many Mafia killings in Bowling Green?"

"This would be our first."

Prine smiled. "Thanks for your input, Officer. Is your chief in?"

"He came back to work after I called in. There's a WTOL crew at the station and I don't know who else. That's why he asked you to meet me here." Her face was flat.

"Good man. Any press at the scene?"

"Just one, a kid from the *Blast.* That's an underground newspaper on campus. She must've had a scanner. I caught her trying to break in the back."

HUE CREW SCREWS BLUES, Prine remembered. "I've heard of the *Blast.* Girl, was it? Did you arrest her?"

"I shooed her away. She's okay, just eager. Anyway I couldn't secure her and the scene at the same time. Someone might've broken in the front while I was reading her rights."

"I hope you're right. Not about what you did, about her being okay. I just signed an authorization to give that paper police credentials."

Alfiero's smile was as pretty as her face.

"There'll be no stopping her now."

He frowned. "Not the answer I was hoping for. Your chief's name is Higgins, isn't it?"

"Harrison, sir."

"That's right, Harrison played Higgins." He didn't wait to be reminded she didn't know Rex Harrison from Carroll O'Connor. "I'd like to talk to him."

"Sir." She unclipped a cellular telephone from among the paraphernalia on her belt, dialed the number and the extension, and handed him the instrument.

When a low-pitched voice answered, "Harrison," Prine said, "Edgar Prine here, Chief. Have you issued a statement?"

"Oh, hello, Captain. I thought it'd be best to wait until I spoke to you."

"Good. When you do, you can tell them you've asked the State Police to help with the investigation."

Brief pause. "I called you out of courtesy. I haven't gotten so far as requesting help."

"That's your decision, of course. It swings on whether you think a mob murder in your jurisdiction is good for the city."

A longer silence followed. "Nothing in the preliminary report suggests the mob was involved."

"Everything I've heard suggests it was."

Harrison's tone underwent a sea change. "It would be different if this homicide is connected with a state investigation," he said. "Naturally, the Bowling Green Police Department stands willing to offer its services to the Armed Robbery Task Force." It sounded like a statement to the press.

"Just for now, say that we're assisting you, and let's not mention the ARTF yet. It's not unusual for a small city force to ask for help from Columbus in a homicide. I'll send a team out to the scene immediately." He hit End and returned the telephone to Rosetta Alfiero. "Thanks, Officer."

She returned it to her belt. She opened her mouth, closed it, opened it again. "Captain? Is the ARTF recruiting anyone from outside the department?"

He studied her from head to foot, nodded. "Ask Columbus for an application form. Send it to the attention of Lieutenant Farrell McCormick at the capitol. They'll forward it." He spelled the name.

"Thanks, Captain." She finished writing, took a deep breath, and let it out, and with it her case of nerves. This was what she'd been working up to.

"Good luck," Prine said. "Now tell me more about the crime scene."

* * *

McCormick was listening to an interview on NPR when Prine slid into the passenger's seat. The lieutenant switched off the radio. "Anything for us?"

"I shouldn't tell you. If you'd gone in with me, that'd be one less time I'd have to repeat it. A strong stomach's supposed to go with the job."

"I scraped my share of high-school kids off telephone poles when I was with Pickaway. That doesn't mean I got used to it. Anyway, Admiral Nelson got seasick every time he shoved off. That didn't stop him from clobbering the French fleet."

"Why can't you listen to sports like other cops?" Prine told him what he'd learned inside, including what Officer Alfiero had said about professional killers.

"She's right," McCormick said. "This guy didn't go there to pop anyone. Maybe he broke in to steal guns and Oster caught him."

"Not trombones?"

"Guns were out in the open, you said. If Oster was in the habit of leaving 'em that way, we'd have busted him before this."

"No sign of B and E; place was locked up tight when the lady cop got there. And burglars surprised in the act don't normally use garrotes. The guns weren't loaded, but he could have grabbed one and cracked Oster's skull. Or a tool from the bench. A good strangling is skilled labor. Contract killers don't burgle. Only another contract killer would have guts enough to suggest it."

"So he went there to buy a gun and something went wrong."

"That's how I read it. Whatever he carried away with him, he sweated for it. Oster wrestled in college — that's probably where he made his gambling contacts — and went pro for six months until some gorilla from Argentina pile-drived him into a compressed vertebra. The girl said the room looked like a tornado hit it. This guy's going to need plenty of BenGay tomorrow."

"What makes it Oster was selling guns to the Color Guard?"

Prine wrinkled his nose at the newspaper tag. "Not a thing, except you can spit here from Toledo, and the job stinks mob hit. Maybe Oster got his cold feet from what went down in Hilliard."

"What's a hitter doing robbing video stores?"

"Economy's gone to pieces. Everybody's scraping to get by. It's still heavyweight work, not the same as punching in windows and groping around in the dark."

"It's a stretch."

"That's why the task force isn't officially involved. Bowling Green can take the fall if it doesn't pan out. Press is all over this one. The city boys love it when Mayberry joins the statistics."

" 'Terror comes to Main Street,' " McCormick said.

" ' "What's become of things," say the locals who gather in the barbershop,' " Prine said.

" 'Folks hereabouts hardly ever lock their doors.' "

"I forgot that one," Prine said. "It's got to be their favorite."

"You think any place was ever like that?"

"Not since cars." The captain smiled. "The lady cop caught a kid from the *Blast* trying to break into the music store."

"Think he's the one wrote that headline?"

"He's a she." A full-size van cruised past the morgue with WTOL-TV painted on the side. "Let's go home before they catch the scent."

McCormick turned on the ignition. "You want me to green-light Alfiero's application?"

"Trash it. Female police officers run against the natural order."

TWENTY

"What if it's a trap?" Laurie asked.

"It could be a trap," Peter said.

"That wasn't the question."

"I'm not invisible. If he wanted to take me out, he could do it anytime, anonymously, from ambush. He doesn't know who I might tell about meeting him at the Alehouse. He'd be making himself a suspect."

She tried to read his expression in the light mounted outside her mother's front door. It was hard enough to read in broad daylight, and fifty more years of marriage wouldn't improve that. It was the first opportunity she'd had to talk to him about the meeting he'd agreed to with Benjamin Grinnell; her mother had ridden in the backseat during the drive back to her house from the Bread Basket.

"He knows for sure *I* know," she said. "Mother, too."

"There were parking attendants and customers who could have overheard. He wasn't whispering. You're not in danger."

"Because we're women?"

"Women haven't been off-limits for years. Maybe never. He needs Pamela; she makes him look legitimate. You're her daughter, so he can't afford to have anything happen to you."

"You're her son-in-law. Does that count?"

"Up to a point. Right now I think he wants to know how much I know about him and what he's up to. That's why I brought up Canada and his real name. I'm pretty sure he won't try anything until he finds out how much I know."

"Pretty sure."

"I don't have a crystal ball."

"You told him almost everything you know with those two questions."

"He doesn't know that."

"Maybe Mother put him up to it. She doesn't trust you."

"Maybe, but he didn't suggest a meeting until after I broke the ice."

"What are you going to tell him?"

"As little as possible, until I find out what he's up to."

"It sounds like two alley cats circling each other in the dark. Then they fight to the death."

"Rarely. Usually one of them has enough and runs away."

"I didn't see anything about him running away in that stuff Loyal Dorfman dug up."

"There weren't any murders, either. Whatever he is, he's not a killer."

"Would you say I'm a killer?"

"You absolutely are not."

"I killed a man." She whispered it.

"He was going to kill you."

"Grinnell probably thinks you're going to kill him. He must, if he knows anything about you at all."

"I don't know what he knows. He and I are in the same boat when it comes to that."

"Don't go," she said. "I don't care what he's up to. If I knew it was going to come to this I never would've asked you to find out."

"It's too late for that."

She hesitated for the first time in the conversation. "Do you have a gun?" She mouthed the question, not making a sound.

He nodded; or she thought he did. It was hard to tell in the dim light with moth shadows fluttering across his face. In any case she knew the answer.

"Bowling Green," she said.

He said nothing.

"All I wanted was to buy my grandfather's farm. I was safe there."

"You're safe now. I won't let anything happen to you."

She shook her head. "Nobody's safe."

They were in each other's arms briefly. Their kiss was hard and short. Then he stepped off the porch and got into the car.

"I bought that black dress for a party," she said.

She couldn't tell if he'd heard. He started the motor and backed out into the street.

The Alehouse occupied one of several plants that had discharged sludge into the Maumee River for fifty years, stood empty for twenty-five, and then been gentrified into lofts and restaurants and community playhouses. In the Popsicle light of a neon sign shaped like a tilted mug spilling foam, BUCKEYE GLASS CO. could still be read in faded letters on a concrete soffit below the flat roof. The river, abused and reclaimed by turns, soughed along behind the building, shucking reflected light like scales.

Macklin parked in an unlighted corner

of the lot with the car pointed toward the street, opened the trunk, lifted the hatch that covered the spare tire in its well, and scooped the Dan Wesson .38 from its hiding place inside the rim. The optional four- and six-inch barrels were there as well, in their Ziploc bag. He left them there, stuck the revolver under his belt in the small of his back, felt to make sure his sport coat hung over it without snagging, and went inside. He was fifteen minutes early, and a little surprised not to find Grinnell waiting for him. It put him more on edge, rather than less. In the business they shared, eleven o'clock always meant 10:45 at the latest.

At that hour on a Saturday night the bar was packed and noisy. He asked his harried young host for a table for two in the dining room. The young man led him to one near the windows looking out on the river, but Macklin pointed to one in a corner.

"Most people prefer the view."

Macklin looked at him. The young man shrugged and carried the menus to the corner table.

The Alehouse was a brewpub. From his seat, Macklin could see the beer-making operation through a glass wall, the gleaming copper-plated cooker and the elaborate pipework and the metal ladders the modern-day brewmeisters climbed carrying their sacks of barley and hops. The history printed on the back of his menu told him the place had brewed beer all through Prohibition for the Detroit Purple Gang, and that the equipment was a faithful, if scaled-down, reproduction of the original. A pen-and-ink drawing of a machine gun–toting character in a fedora with one foot propped on the running board of a bug-eyed sedan decorated the front of the menu. Macklin wondered what the half-life was of a criminal stigma before it became a selling point.

"Am I late? I was under the impression I was a bit early."

Macklin had seen Grinnell coming from across the room, a trim man fighting middle age with a crisp walk, wearing the hand-crocheted open-weave sweater he'd had on earlier, over a button-down white Oxford shirt and pleated slacks. He looked like an instructor at a state university hoping to look like a Harvard professor. It was a neat bit of double subterfuge, fully appreciated only by another who'd lived life in imitation of something else. He rose and shook Grinnell's hand. If the man was armed, he'd put it in the same place

Macklin had, behind his back and out of sight.

"We're both early," Macklin said. "The traffic wasn't as bad as I thought it would be."

"Remind yourself of that in an hour, when you're stuck in a jam heading out of town. Are you eating?"

"No, but go ahead and order. All you had was half a carrot cake."

"I ate at home earlier. What will you drink?"

"Gin highball." He hated gin. He could nurse it for an hour.

When a waitress appeared, wearing an old-fashioned bartender's striped shirt with sleeve garters, Grinnell gave her the menus and ordered the gin highball and a Scotch and soda for himself.

"Belated congratulations on your marriage," he said when she left. "You have a beautiful and intelligent wife."

"She takes after her mother."

Grinnell accepted that as a compliment to himself. "Pamela's been good for me. I led a rootless life before her. But I suppose you know that."

Their drinks came. When they were alone again, Grinnell lifted his. "To the ladies."

Macklin sipped his gin. The bartender had mixed it with Canada Dry. He was used to Vernor's, but he welcomed the flatter agent. It would slow his consumption that much more.

"I won't ask your methods," Grinnell said. "My naturalization is a matter of public record. Anyone can find out my birth name. The question is why."

"You overplayed your hand. You were so dull you made yourself interesting."

"Laurie put you up to it, I suppose. The cub protects the sow."

"Something like that."

"Would you be insulted if I said I didn't believe you?"

"You overplayed it again. If I would be, you couldn't ask that question without insulting me."

"Suppose I didn't care."

"Everything all right with your drinks?"

Neither of them looked at the waitress. Grinnell said, "Fine, fine," and she coasted over to the next inhabited table.

"Macklin isn't an uncommon name," Grinnell said then. "I didn't make any connections at first. A man I used to work for had an associate in Detroit. This fellow employed a man to clean up messes. That man's name was Macklin. I never heard his

Christian name. Men in that line of work usually pick up a colorful moniker, Icepick Pete or Mack the Smack, but I never heard that either."

"Those nicknames are usually invented by newspaper reporters. If he was any good, he never made the papers."

"I assume he was good. Otherwise, he'd be dead or in prison by now."

"You don't know he isn't."

Grinnell drank. "Suppose we turn over a card."

"I used to work in Detroit," Macklin said. "I retired at forty."

"How did you manage that? I didn't think Detroit offered a package."

"It gets easier when you outlive your employers."

"Ah."

Macklin took another swallow. "Your turn."

"I may give you information you already have."

"If you do, I'll tell you."

Grinnell shook his head, smiling. "That's just a cheap way of drawing a card you don't have coming."

"I'm tired of talking about cards."

"So am I." He turned his glass around in its wet ring on the napkin. "I shaded the truth some when I said I used to work for that man I told you about, the one who knew the man in Detroit. I answer to his son, but technically he's still my boss."

"In Toledo?"

"Yes."

"Toledo's Joe Vulpo's town."

"Detroit was Mike Boniface's."

"A long time ago."

"After that it was Carlo Maggiore's," Grinnell said. "He was killed last year in L.A."

"That's what I heard."

Grinnell lifted his glass, then sipped. "I guess that means I'm up. When I told you I was a facilitator, I wasn't lying. I go out ahead and make sure things go smoothly for those who come after."

"What happens then?"

"Things go smoothly," he said. "Most of the time, anyway."

"When was the last time they didn't?"

Grinnell shook his head again.

"Another question," Macklin said. "It doesn't have anything to do with our agreement."

"I'll have to be the judge of that."

"Are you wearing a wire?"

Grinnell's left eye twitched. Macklin was pretty sure he'd surprised him. "I'm not, but of course I could be lying. Are you?"

"Same answer."

"You son of a bitch!" Grinnell spat. He shoved his glass off the edge of the table.

It burst into pieces when it struck the hardwood floor. A piece of glass or a drop of liquid hit Macklin's pants leg. Heads swiveled their way from the other tables. The waitress, waiting for someone's order at the bar, looked, then signaled the bartender. He disappeared behind the back bar, then came out and handed her a broom and dustpan and a towel. She hastened over. Grinnell and Macklin watched each other in silence.

"Accident? Anyone splashed?" The waitress looked from one man to the other.

"My fault," Grinnell said. "We're both okay. I'm very sorry."

"No problem. I'll get you another drink." She squatted and used the broom like a whisk, then mopped up the spill with the towel. She left carrying it and the broom and the laden dustpan.

Grinnell said, "Sorry about the outburst. Obviously, if one of us were lying, we'd be up to our necks in civil servants by now."

"Does that mean we can stop talking in code?"

"Better than that. We can start talking."

The waitress brought him another Scotch and soda. He handed her a five-dollar bill.

She held it as if she didn't know what it was. "That's not necessary, sir. Replacements are on the house."

"A good policy. There's another five coming if you can manage to ignore us until last call."

The waitress complied.

The man seated on the passenger's side of the Ford Crown Victoria touched the arm of the man behind the wheel, who said, "Yeah," and held out his hand for the camera.

The driver's name was Barlow, and he was a sergeant with the Armed Robbery Task Force, recruited personally from highway patrol by Lieutenant Farrell McCormick shortly after the lieutenant's own transfer from the Pickaway County Sheriff's Department. Barlow had come with a jacket full of commendations and a dislike for public attention, both important points to Captain Prine, who'd come to the detail with neither. No one else in the detail had logged more hours on stakeout than the sergeant.

He balanced the telephoto lens on the

edge of his window, which when Grinnell entered the Alehouse he'd raised to the level where he could shoot straight and comfortably when his subject came out. The instrument was new, a digital model with an ultraviolet lens, and would have set him back two months' pay if it didn't belong to the State of Ohio.

When Grinnell emerged alone, Barlow took several shots of him descending the short flight of steps to the parking lot. Columbus already knew what Grinnell looked like; he was merely establishing the location, with the camera providing an automatic time stamp. He watched Grinnell climb up into his rented four-wheeler and pull out into the street, but did not start the car to follow.

His partner said nothing. The young man, whose name was Freeland, was new to the ARTF, a former third-grade detective with the city police in Sandusky who'd come to the capital with a letter of recommendation from a state senator — a long-time Prine ally — and had the virtue of keeping his mouth shut pending explanation. Barlow had an idea he'd work out if he could keep his ambition in check.

Grinnell had been gone three minutes when another man came outside, looked around, and trotted down the steps. It seemed that his gaze had lighted on the Crown Victoria for a half beat, and the sergeant, who had parked under the scaffolding of the warehouse undergoing renovation next door, shrank back into the shadows that filled the car; but after that infinitesimal pause the man behaved as if the car were invisible.

Barlow recognized him from the restaurant in Myrtle, where he'd had to set up surveillance on foot because there was no unobtrusive place to park within sight of the entrance, and leave the camera and Freeland down the street. The man's face was as unfamiliar as it was unremarkable, but there had been conversation between the two while they were waiting for their vehicles and Barlow had memorized the features of the two women who joined them after a few minutes. The women had then gotten into the stranger's car and Barlow had had to sprint for the Ford in order to follow Grinnell. There was no sign of either of the women at the brewpub.

Barlow took three quick shots of the man walking and, as he pulled out of his slot, two of the Michigan license plate, a standard issue with no commemoratives.

The car was the last model of the Mercury Cougar, a forgettable design with a reliable plant under the hood.

He didn't follow the car. After the tail-lights winked out behind the corner of the warehouse, he broke the disc out of the camera and fed it into the scanner built into the onboard computer. Technology he didn't understand would whisk the jumble of pixels to Columbus, where whoever had the duty could deal with the Secretary of State's office in Michigan and match the car to the man. He plopped the camera onto Freeland's lap, turned the key, and went in search of Grinnell.

TWENTY-ONE

"Who's Myrtle?" Francis Spain asked. "I thought the manager's name was Pam."

"Pamela." His publicist, Becca Jacobetti, sighed genteely, using only her nostrils. She was a trim ash-blonde who wore designer glasses in pewter frames and a steel-colored suit with a shimmer that in another time, on a man, Spain would have called sharkskin. He wondered, if he used the description in a book, if his readers would consider him old hat. "It's a what, not a who. It's the name of the town where we're going."

They were cruising west on I-80 in a champagne-colored stretch limo with beige leather upholstery and a dwarf bar built into the passenger door. The driver, an eyebrowless wonder named Kevin, wearing an electric-blue blazer, had picked them up at Toledo Express Airport. Sixteen-city tour, a fortune spent on first-class fare and hotel suites, and Kevin had to meet them with Spain's name written in black Magic

Marker on a piece of corrugated fiberboard torn from a carton. He'd had half a mind to ignore it and call a cab, but Becca had walked right up to the man and handed him her garment bag.

And now he found out that one of the sixteen cities was Hooterville.

"I was told Toledo," he said. "That's the other way."

"*Greater* Toledo. These days, readers go out to the suburbs. There's nothing like a roomy bookstore in a shopping center on a rainy Saturday. They line up like poor people."

"The sun is shining. In case you hadn't noticed."

"Relax, Francis. You saw the *Times* list. Number Two ain't shabby."

"That fucking Grisham. When's he going to take a break, give someone else a shot?"

"I've represented writers who've been waiting their whole careers just for a *review.* You cracked the list with your first book. By the end of this tour you'll be locked in for life."

"I can live without their reviews. Last week Danielle Steele called me 'the ten-thousand-and-first monkey.' I don't even know what that means."

Becca smiled briefly, then pursed her lips. "It's a literary reference. A mathematical one, actually. You know: If you leave ten thousand monkeys in a room with ten thousand word processors, sooner or later one of them will write a novel."

"I knew it was some sort of slam. I didn't see *Mistral's Daughter* on the syllabus at Princeton."

"That was Judith Krantz. I wouldn't lose any sleep over it."

"Of course not. You're not the one she called a monkey."

"Last week's *Time* is lining birdcages, and *Serpent in Eden* is in every airport from Sydney to Savannah. No one in Hollywood's in any hurry to option Balzac."

"Fuck Hollywood. Warner Brothers had me escorted off the *Love Song* set just because I caught them straying from the script. That script was damn faithful to the original."

"You told me they wrote out the lounge singer."

"I might've said something about that, too. I don't remember. There's a cow. Jesus." He was staring out the window. "What happened to the Little Professor?"

"You found out they were stacking *Serpent* back in the Romance section and wrote an e-mail to the publisher. I called the vice president of the chain, he gave me the runaround, and I pulled all your signings with them. There weren't that many, and others have stepped up to plug the holes. That's how we got Myrtle. I'd already confirmed the tickets, so here we are. The cow probably won't show up."

"Funny. Do they have people as funny as you at William Morrow?"

"Probably. They publish Patsy Cornwell." She patted his hand. Hers wore an engagement ring. He had yet to meet a woman under thirty in publishing who wasn't getting married, just married, or going through a divorce; the turnover was worse than in Hollywood. "You'll have a good time, I promise. They don't get to see many big-ticket authors out here, and here's where the sales are. Winter lasts five months. They've got nothing to do but shovel snow and read."

He withdrew his hand and turned back toward the window. They were passing one of those high walls built to keep expressway noise from reaching residents, probably a trailer park. "I don't like independents. They all smell like old magazines and they treat me like an idiot because I'm not starving."

"This one's part of a small chain." She lifted the flap on her briefcase and retrieved a computer printout from among the papers inside. "The manager's serving champagne and canapés before the signing. She's invited some local dignitaries. She wouldn't go to that kind of trouble if she thought you were an idiot. I don't know what she smells like."

"I can see it now: bunch of pig farmers in new overalls and a mayor with a red sash across his chest. What about security?" He'd begun getting anonymous letters comparing him to the serpent in Eden, offering to sing a love song at his funeral.

She lowered the printout and pressed a button in her armrest. "Kevin? Mr. Spain asked about security."

The smoked-glass partition separating passengers from driver slid down noiselessly into a pocket. Without taking his eyes from the road, the eyebrowless wonder snapped something loose from under his blazer, held up a square semiautomatic pistol with a brushed-steel finish, and returned it to its place.

"Kevin's with Heartland Protection out of Chicago," Becca said. "He used to be an air marshal."

"Bugged out after nine-one-one, that it?"

But Spain couldn't keep from sounding impressed.

"I left three years ago. They asked me to come back, but I'm allergic to pretzels." The driver slid the partition back up without waiting for a response.

"Just a precaution," Becca said. "Writers are the Ford Escort of hot lists. These days it's more dangerous teaching high school."

"Tell that to Salman Whatsizname."

The publicist wasn't listening. She was moving her lips over the printout, committing the information to memory. Finally she looked up and stuffed it back into her briefcase. "Here's Myrtle. See? No overalls."

Dueling Texaco stations, an Arby's, a KFC, and Kinko's glided past on either side of a broad avenue without cracks or joins in the asphalt; square yellow flags stuck up where the lines had yet to be painted. Everything looked new enough to come with a freshness date. Spain felt the tension draining out through the soles of his feet. People who went to restaurants where they'd already memorized the menus were people who read books like *Love Song* and *Serpent in Eden*. He wondered why Becca hadn't gone ahead and told him that and spared him the effort of complaining.

* * *

The little black dress hung from the folding louvered door of the hotel-room closet, where Laurie could see it reflected in the bathroom mirror where she was applying the top coat on her makeup. When she turned her head one way and then back, glimpsing the dress in the corner of her eye, she thought at first it was a woman standing there. She'd been spooking that way for a week.

"What's going to happen today?" she asked.

"Your mother's going to sell a ton of books, if she doesn't explode first." Paper crackled. Peter had finished dressing, everything except his suit coat, and was sitting on the bed, reading *USA Today* with a pillow bunched behind his back and his legs stretched out on the bedspread to keep the seams of his trousers straight. She couldn't see him, but that was what he always did in a hotel room when he got ready ahead of her, which was another thing he always did. Men had it easy.

This time there'd been no nonsense about Mother persuading them to stay at her house. She was a fistful of nerves with Francis Spain already on the ground and two hours to showtime. Laurie had just gotten off the telephone with her.

"I don't mean what's going to happen with Mother. I mean Benjamin."

"Probably nothing. He works for the Vulpos. You're always safe around an organization man. Unless you work for the organization. It's like having a policeman on the corner."

"You don't believe that."

"I believed him when he said he's getting out. That's what you wanted me to find out."

"What if they don't want him out? The Vulpos, I mean. You said they're crazy."

"That's the rumor. Joe's senile and they say Tommy likes to dress up like a woman. Personally I think he's just getting in touch with his feminine side."

"You make me nervous when you joke. You don't have that much of a sense of humor." She started to put on mascara, but her hand was shaking. She put down the brush and picked up her lipstick. Better to get Bermuda Pink on her teeth than stick herself in the eye.

"He was worried about me and I was worried about him. Turned out we both thought the other one was spying for the organization. He's in the same place I was three years ago. That broke the ice. You and I have already had this conversation."

"So with Mother and Benjamin it's like it is with me and you."

"That's how I see it."

"Then why do you still have that gun?"

They hadn't talked about the gun since the night he'd gone to meet Grinnell at the brewpub in Toledo. He'd hardly hoped she'd forgotten it, but she might have assumed he'd gotten rid of it. She knew he didn't keep them around unless he had something specific in mind. Hanging onto unregistered firearms had sent more hitters to prison than the reasons they'd hung onto them in the first place.

"What makes you think I still have it?" he asked. That month's hot Hollywood couple beamed out at him from the front page of the entertainment section.

"It never takes you longer than three minutes to put the bags in the trunk when we leave someplace. It took you five when we left Mother's. Where do you put it, with the spare tire?"

He turned the page. "I didn't know you were timing me."

"Peter."

"I couldn't very well leave it at your mother's. I'll dump it in the stream behind the house next time we go there. The silt's as deep as I am tall."

Something rattled and clanked; Laurie nearly knocking over one of her bottles or jars. They filled every square inch of counter space, and when she came out she looked the same as she had when she'd gone in. "We promised each other no more secrets."

"I know."

He said it as sincerely as possible. He'd meant it when he'd promised it, but in practice it was a promise impossible to keep. If he kept it, told her everything all the time, she'd be in a constant state of nervous collapse. Laurie was one young woman in a million, tougher than some men whose toughness he'd admired when he was still young enough to admire that sort of thing, but she hadn't spent a lifetime on the wall, learned to deaden her senses, like a fighter soaking his hands in brine to thicken the skin on his knuckles and kill the nerves beneath. You had to die a little to avoid death. That was something he could never explain to her without killing what they had.

He hadn't told her, for instance, that Grinnell had changed the subject both times Macklin had mentioned the bookstore signing, or that Grinnell's conversation about his future never went beyond the coming week — the week just gone. The man had been full of questions about how Macklin had managed to leave the Detroit Combination, and because his curiosity had tipped his hand, had been candid about his own wishes to get out from under, but as to an innocuous promotional event that had nothing to do with how he'd made his living, he'd merely said that was Pamela's department and his only contribution was to stay out of the way until it came time to show his support by showing his face.

It was clear Grinnell's only motive in arranging their meeting was to find out whom Macklin represented. Having established to his own satisfaction that he represented no one, his interest was in the details of Macklin's escape from Detroit. Well, Macklin had been less than forthcoming about that, avoiding specifics; and so the conversation had been frustrating on both sides.

Nor had Macklin mentioned to Laurie the surveillance car he'd spotted on his way out of the Alehouse. Everything about it, from the make and model to its location, in the shadow of a scaffolding on the far edge of a nearly deserted parking lot, assured him he wasn't just being paranoid. Whether the car had been following him or Grinnell, whoever had been inside knew by now who Macklin was, and so did his superiors.

He hadn't told Laurie either of these things, because if she suspected something was going to happen at the signing, she'd have tried to get her mother to call it off, and she couldn't do that without raising questions neither she nor Macklin could answer without blowing the top off the world they were trying to build. Or she would insist on notifying the police. The police would be there in any case, he was sure of that. And so would someone else. In life as in nature, natural enemies attracted one another.

Laurie closed the door to use the bathroom. She was shy about that, despite her nurse's training and being married a year. When the ventilator fan began whirring, Macklin put the paper aside, got up, and slid the Dan Wesson .38 from between the two fat telephone books in the bottom drawer of the dresser built into the wall. He checked the cylinder, nestled the butt into the small of his back, put on his suit coat, and inspected his profile in the full-length mirror for bulges. He'd never been to an autograph party and didn't want to embarrass his escort.

TWENTY-TWO

It was Independence Day, but Wild Bill wasn't just sure how to declare it.

He'd had his fill of Toledo. When Jesse James, his man Jesse, took it in his head to tip over a bank or a train, he didn't wire St. Louis for permission, and he sure wouldn't put up with somebody like Carlos.

"Hey, man, they got a snack machine here?" Carlos asked. "I need a Baby Ruth."

Mark Twain said, "Baby Ruth looks like a turd. You put turds in your mouth?"

"Hey, I don't do drugs. Take enough of them parrot pills, you jump out the window and try to fly."

"You don't need no windows with the pills. You fly anyway."

"All's I'm saying is I keep the body clean. A little sugar now and then when I need the buzz." He was sitting in the stiff-upholstered armchair with his feet on the bed in black high-top sneakers, drumming his fingers on the Sig Sauer in his lap. The greasy little fucker hadn't let go of it since

Wild Bill had handed out the weapons. Wild Bill liked guns as much as the next man, as much as any Westerner, but Carlos was psycho on the subject.

"I don't call eating turds keeping the body clean."

"There's something down the hall," Wild Bill said. "Leave the piece here. I don't want you shooting up the machine when it swallows your dollar."

"Man, I never paid a dollar for a candy bar in my life."

He was cheap, too.

Wild Bill looked at Donny, Donny leaning on his hands on the table that did double duty as a writing desk and breakfast surface, studying the Wood County road map he'd spread out on it. Donny was all business. Wild Bill had never even seen him eat before a job.

Carlos got up finally, slapped the pistol down on the bed, and went out the hallway door. Mark Twain came up off the love seat and switched off the Weather Channel. "Let's clear out before he comes back."

Wild Bill grinned in response and thumped a finger down on a secondary road. "Don't forget they're tearing up that stretch."

Donny said, "Tell me about it. The whole state of Ohio's under construction."

"You'd think they'd check with us first."

They were all in a room on Motel Row in Harbor View, place with the biggest most ornate lobby Wild Bill had ever seen outside Denver, supported by a shuttle-service arrangement with the amusement park in Cedar Point. The woodwork alone had set somebody back twenty grand, but he'd made up for it by stocking the rooms with just basic cable and Handi Wipes for towels. There were no moisturizers or shoe mitts and you could crack ice on the so-called queen-size mattress. A lightbulb was burned out. Wild Bill figured *Ramada* was Spanish for cheapshit. Nobody ever sat at a table in McDonald's more than twenty minutes and nobody ever stayed in one of those cardboard rooms more than one night at a time. Check 'em in, check 'em out, make room for the next poor dumb tired son of a bitch lugging his ballbuster wife and squealing brats ten hours round-trip from Kalamazoo.

The ideal place for four desperados to put up their heels before taking someplace down.

Mark Twain said, "You think this guy'll write a book about it after?"

"He don't write that kind of book. Maybe when Lawrence Block signs."

"I'm in a book." Mark closed his eyes. "*Recidivism and Racism: A Study of Serial Criminal Behavior in North America Post-Brown v. the Board of Education*. Midget professor from the University of Michigan interviewed me in Jackson. I got most of a page."

"Yeah?" Wild Bill said. "Who's playing you in the movie?"

"Go fuck yourself. You even know what a recidivist is?"

"I think we're doing it today."

Someone knocked at the door that led from the parking lot. There was a wad of paper stuffed in the broken peephole, but Wild Bill looked around the curtain in the big window next to the door and saw Ben Grinnell standing there in a suit. He leaned the shotgun against the radiator, twisted the latch, and opened the door.

"What's it today, in or out?" Wild Bill said.

"I'm here, so I guess it's in. Do you want this in the room or out in the parking lot?"

"If you're talking about the lay, I got it. Busy little store. I guess everybody's not home loving Lucy."

"What do you know about security?"

"There's *nada*. Book people spook too easy. You ever try to browse through *Penthouse* with some semipro breathing peppermint over your shoulder?"

"Spain's bringing a bodyguard. His name's Kevin Randle, with an *l-e*. Former air marshal, three-year man with Heartland Protection. They pave the way for the Secret Service whenever the president comes through chasing votes."

Wild Bill stepped out of the way. "Enter, brother. You want a candy bar?"

Grinnell was no longer driving either the rented SUV or his Lexus. He'd risen early that morning, put on the midnight-blue Brooks Brothers suit he'd picked out for the autograph party, took one last look around at his condominium, and driven downtown to his bank. There he opened his safe deposit box and distributed fifteen thousand dollars in bricks of hundreds among his pockets. The box was still two-thirds full when he returned it.

He'd driven from there down to Cincinnati to exchange the SUV for the car. On the way he stopped to fill the tank and call a number in Mason from the pay telephone in the station. He was told an hour would be needed to make the arrangements he'd requested.

The Lexus was still parked in the free space where he'd left it. He hadn't bothered with evasive tactics on the way there, knowing he'd just have to repeat them when he picked up the car and with it the police unit assigned to it. He drove it to Mason and an automatic car wash whose owner was still paying off the interest on a loan made by Joe Vulpo in 1993. Once inside, and between the soap and the rinse, Grinnell got out and climbed into another car on its way to the drying cycle. It was a four-year-old black Ford Taurus, the linear opposite of a new frost-green Lexus. On the front seat he found the nylon duffel he'd asked for and a fisherman's canvas bucket hat, a nice touch. He clapped on the hat. When the man in coveralls at the exit finished hand-buffing the fenders and mirrors, Grinnell rolled down the window and handed him ten thousand dollars. The man was the owner of the car wash and a used-car dealership in Loveland.

In his rearview mirror, Grinnell watched the owner step into the office and emerge after less than a minute without the coveralls and smoothing the creases out of a blue suit with his hands. He got into the Lexus. The ten thousand would be waiting for him inside after the state police were through grilling him. The Taurus certainly wasn't worth that much. With any luck, the police wouldn't become suspicious and pull the Lexus over for hours.

Back in Toledo, Grinnell had parked the Taurus near his bank, taken off the hat, signed out his box for the second time that day, and placed the remaining sixty-five thousand dollars in the nylon duffel. Then he'd driven straight from there to the Ramada Inn in Harbor View.

Wild Bill and the others were wearing identical red sport shirts. They looked like a bowling team.

After letting him in, Wild Bill sat on the bed, picked up an antique revolver Grinnell hadn't seen before from the nightstand, and twirled it forward and backward on his trigger finger like a character in an old western. The weapon looked rusty and nonfunctional. Grinnell supposed it was a good-luck piece.

"What's this Randle look like?" Wild Bill asked.

"I've never seen him. I got the information secondhand."

The long-haired man grinned. "I had a secondhand boat once. Set me back a season's pay. First time I took it out on Flathead Lake, it sprung a leak. I had to swim for my life *and* pay two hundred bucks to the sheriff to get it off the bottom."

"My source can be trusted."

"Mine, too. She works the cash register in the bookstore."

Grinnell said nothing.

The black man named Mark Twain clicked his tongue. "I think you stuck him, bro. Man's paler than usual."

"We went out for sinkers and coffee," Wild Bill said. "Town's growing; they got a Krispy Kreme out by the expressway. The manager don't tell the help shit, but my little redhead saw someone pick her up at the curb a couple of times. Man drives a Lexus and don't exactly look like someone who couldn't be you." He stopped twirling with the muzzle pointed at Grinnell's midsection. "You should've told me before you had it on with the boss lady. I'd've understood why you wanted to bug out."

"That's the other thing I was going to tell you," Grinnell said. "I'll be there today."

"Was you going to tell me before I told you about the little redhead?"

"Hey, it's Lord Butthole. I thought you upped and quit."

Grinnell looked briefly at the Hispanic

named Carlos, who'd come in from the hall holding a half-eaten candy bar with the wrapper skinned down like the peel on a banana. The fourth man, the quiet one who drove, hadn't looked up from the map in front of him since Grinnell had entered.

To Wild Bill, Grinnell said, "As a matter of fact, I was. I couldn't risk surprising you."

"What about the guy your girlfriend's daughter's hooked up with? He be there too?"

Grinnell didn't hesitate. He'd assumed the man had found out most of the superficial details. "He's invited. His name's Macklin. I don't know him very well."

"He a cop?"

"He was in the camera business. He's retired."

Wild Bill resumed twirling, forward, then backward; smacking the butt into his palm between revolutions.

"That straight?"

"It's what he told Pamela."

"You believe him?"

"I said I don't know him very well."

"I guess you ain't such of a much of a judge of character."

"It must be the company I've been keeping."

"We need this guy?" Carlos asked.

Wild Bill ignored him. "I hope this isn't another secondhand boat. If it is, your girlfriend's coming out of there with a face full of double-O."

"You don't have that option after Hilliard."

"I got five options in the magazine and one in the barrel."

Grinnell said, "You've also got the State Police Task Force on one side and Tommy Vulpo on the other. This isn't a western."

"What'd I just say?"

Carlos popped the rest of the candy bar into his mouth and crumpled the wrapper. "Why not do him right here? One less place to look when we hit the store."

Wild Bill stopped twirling. His moustache lifted away from his teeth. "I can't see any holes in it. How about you?"

Grinnell watched him.

"Didn't think so." Wild Bill pulled the trigger. The hammer snapped on an empty chamber.

Maybe a broken firing pin. Grinnell relaxed his arm. He'd jerked it behind his back when the hammer fell.

Mark Twain laughed. Grinnell had never heard him do that. He wondered if he was on drugs.

Grinnell left. In the Taurus, he checked inside the duffel, then took the Browning BDA out from under his belt and put it inside with the cash. It was an uncomfortable thing to haul around until you needed it.

Carlos said, "You should of popped him."

"Man was carrying, couldn't you tell?" Wild Bill said. "He had more'n a stick up his ass this time."

"You had the drop. That cowboy piece of shit even work?"

Wild Bill stood, stuck Uncle Jakey's fake Colt inside his waistband, and dropped the tail of his sport shirt over it. He always felt indestructible when he had it on him; he was sure it would prove to be his bluff card in the hole someday. "Speaking of shit," he said. "We ain't stopping this time."

Carlos went into the bathroom and shut the door. His stomach always got bad on a working day. It was probably the fucking Baby Ruths.

Wild Bill waved Mark over and murmured in his ear. He didn't like to distract Donny with details from inside.

Mark nodded. "How you want to divvy 'em up?"

"I better get Grinnell and this Macklin. It's a shotgun job. You take the bodyguard and the boss lady. Bodyguard first."

"Well, sure." Then Mark tipped his head toward the bathroom, lifting his eyebrows.

The toilet flushed. Wild Bill picked up a pillow. When Carlos came out, buckling his belt, Wild Bill scooped up Carlos's Sig Sauer from the bed and shot him twice through the pillow. Bits of foam rubber sprayed out.

Donny jerked his head up in time to see Carlos slide down the doorjamb into a sitting position on the floor. He looked from Carlos to Wild Bill.

"Didn't wash his hands." Wild Bill wiped the pistol on the pillow, dropped them on the bed, and went over to get his shotgun while Mark came forward to fold Donny's map. The room smelled like burning tires.

TWENTY-THREE

During the press conference in the show office, the guardians of the Fourth Estate learned that Lieutenant McCormick had programmed his cell phone to play the theme to *Felix the Cat* when a call came in.

"Thought I had it on vibrate," he muttered, and went through the door to the working office in back to take it.

The laughter turned nervous and smoldered out, extinguished by the heavy theme of justice in the room.

"Lew." Prine pointed at Lewis Wagner.

The statehouse reporter from the *Columbus Dispatch* had a high, professorial forehead and the mean little eyes of a street swindler. It was rumored he'd turned down promotion to managing editor twice because he preferred to see his name on the front page rather than buried in the flag inside. Prine suspected he'd started the rumor himself. He knew for a fact Wagner was the governor's choice for press secretary in the event of his reelection. In the event he lost, the corporate chain that owned the paper wouldn't risk alienating his successor by moving Wagner to management.

"When are you going to give us the name of this suspect you keep hinting about? Is it Yehudi?" The reporter had a yappy little tenor with a crack in it.

"No, Lew, and you're dating yourself. For the record, we never said he was a suspect. At this point he's a possible witness, and he's not in custody. The young man in back." He pointed again.

"Philip Case, *Toledo Blade*." The speaker wore his brown hair in a neat ponytail and round spectacles tinted pink. He read from a steno pad in one hand. "Has there been any progress in the investigation into the possible connection between the Color Guard and Al-Qaeda operatives working in the U.S.?"

"None whatsoever."

"Would you care to explain why?"

"Certainly. No such connection is suspected or ever was. Your editor made it up to sell papers."

"Confidential sources —"

"Confidence *men*," Prine interrupted. "Or women. I don't like to slight either sex."

There was some grumbling in response to this. Not much; Wagner was scarcely more popular among his colleagues than he was with the Armed Robbery Task Force.

"Hello, Ken," Prine said, indicating Ken Abelard with his chin.

Abelard, weekend anchorman and full-time stand-up for WTOL-TV in Toledo, showed his caps and dropped his voice a full octave from its normal speaking range for the benefit of his sound man.

"No one's heard from the Color Guard in weeks," he said. "This is the longest interval between robberies since the spree began. Is it possible, because of the shooting in Hilliard, that the gang has broken up or moved on, and if so, what impact will that have on the success of your investigation?" He got it all out in one breath.

"Anything's possible, Ken. We're working on a more definite solution."

"What steps are you taking to secure it?"

"Well, I can't be specific without giving these creeps an early Christmas present. I will say we aren't just sitting around waiting for them to retire or get up the gumption to rob another video store. Our forensics team is still analyzing evidence from Hilliard and the previous robberies and our investigators are still interviewing witnesses. What you're seeing is just the tip of the iceberg, and this crew is the *Titanic*."

Abelard looked smug. He had his sound bite, and so had Prine.

The captain hurried the other journalists along. He'd peaked early, and after fielding some softball questions from the more sympathetic reporters in the room he was about to wrap up the conference when McCormick came back in and whispered in his ear.

Prine's expression didn't change. He nodded to one of the thick-shouldered plainclothesmen, who placed a hand on the shoulder nearest him and steered the owner gently toward the door to reception. The other plainclothesmen followed suit. Wagner tried to yap one more question, but Prine thanked the reporters loudly and preceded McCormick into the workroom.

He shut the door and glowered at his lieutenant. "Give me it again."

"That was Barlow on the phone. He and young Freeland lost Grinnell four hours ago. He switched vehicles in a car wash in Mason. They were following the wrong man in the right car until a little while ago."

"Arrest him?"

"Guy named Pollard, owns the car wash. City cops busted him year before last for running a book in the back. Did six months in County and paid a fine. He has connections to Joe Vulpo. Think he's talking?"

"What about the condo?"

"I just got off the phone with the detail. They haven't seen Grinnell since he went out early this morning. Barlow and Freeland followed him from there. He made a stop at his bank before he left town. There's more." He handed Prine a fax sheet.

The captain read it swiftly, then again more slowly. It had been sent to his office by a civilian clerical worker assigned to monitor police reports wired from throughout the state and forward items of specific interest. It was a transcript of radio communications with Harbor View Police dispatch involving a fatal shooting at a Ramada Inn there. The dead man was a Hispanic dressed in sneakers, jeans, and a red shirt. The weapon found at the scene was a Sig Sauer 9mm semiautomatic pistol, fired recently, with two cartridges missing from the magazine.

"So it's red this time," Prine said.

"Could be unrelated. Plenty of Sigs floating around out there."

"Who's on Macklin?" The Michigan Secretary of State's office had identified the owner of the license plate Barlow had photographed at the Alehouse a week before, and Prine had ordered surveillance based on Macklin's police and FBI files.

"Crosley."

"Call him."

McCormick got the number from his cellular index and punched it in. He spoke, listened for twenty seconds, then flipped the telephone shut. "He's at the bookstore in Myrtle. Reception for a visiting author."

"They changed their MO."

"If they didn't, we've got a good chance of looking like idiots."

"Radio the Toledo post, tell them we're coming. Call up every man. Hard hats and vests." Prine's smile was bolted down tight. "We might as well dress the part."

TWENTY-FOUR

Laurie had never seen so many boring people gathered in one place.

They weren't even the honest bores of her youth: farmers with sixth-grade educations and no conversation that didn't involve crops and equipment, country wives who cooked all day at the grange hall and never quite got rid of the smell of hot grease, townsmen in loud sport coats who chewed toothpicks and referred to the two hardware stores they owned as a "chain." Those were bores by circumstances, who could not be held responsible for how they turned out. These were self-made.

She couldn't remember if the man who was talking to her belonged to the school board or the county planning commission. He'd been holding forth about temporary classrooms and housing for ten minutes, oblivious to the fact that she hadn't opened her mouth once to encourage him. His black double-breasted suit, blue pinstripe shirt with white collar, and yellow tie all screamed 1985 and appeared to be wearing him rather than the other way around; he had a small, egg-shaped head balanced on a tubular neck and there was space between it and his collar.

It had been this way at every cocktail party she'd ever attended. She supposed it was her fault for looking the way she did. Her blonde hair, good skin, and narrow waist in the simple black dress always drew these types away from their wives with their raccoon eyes and globs of jewelry, and she had never been the kind of woman who could tell a wolf on the make to get lost. Not even the kind of wolf with a line more polished than the statistics on local population growth. She drew a deep breath, let it out, pasted the smile back on her face, and looked to see where Peter had landed.

She found him standing on the edge of the crowd around the guest of honor, holding a flute in which the champagne level hadn't changed since he'd accepted it. Her own was empty, and she wished he'd look over and notice and offer to refill it. He had on the charcoal suit she'd picked out for him, with the almost nonexistent violet stripe that made him look younger, less stodgy than the solid colors he preferred. His wardrobe was the only thing about him she would ever be able to change.

Spain said something that made the group chuckle. Peter flashed his teeth accommodatingly, but his eyes were moving, and she knew from experience that although he'd heard every word and could repeat it back if asked, it had no meaning for him.

Meeting Spain would have been a disappointment if Laurie hadn't already made up her mind about him based on his writing. It was a novelty to shake hands with a man who didn't react to her looks. He'd barely made eye contact, muttered some sort of greeting in the tone teenagers used when they said, "Whatever," and looked right past her toward the next hand to shake, leaving his publicist to introduce herself. To Peter he'd said nothing, but then Peter hadn't offered his hand, had just said, "How do you do?" when Pamela presented him. Spain would always be the center of his own orbit. Laurie had taken herself off to meet some other bore.

Her mother was deeper in the crowd, separated from Spain only by the publicist, who was Laurie's only serious competition in the room, although her business attire gave Laurie the edge. Pamela, in pale green chiffon with a frothy collar that hid the lines in her neck, laughed longer than everyone else at whatever the writer had said and raised a hand often to smooth back her hair, which was too short to need smoothing. It wasn't the first time Laurie had been embarrassed for her mother. She was born to rotate around people like Francis Spain.

Benjamin stood near the door, looking almost distinguished in a midnight blue suit, but otherwise as much a part of the furniture as the full-size cutout of Spain that stood behind a dump rack filled with copies of *Serpent in Eden* in cardboard pockets. The picture had been blown up from the photo on the back of the jacket and had come special delivery from the publisher in New York. Benjamin was holding a glass and listening to a fat woman in purple organdy who had introduced herself to Laurie as the president of the Friends of the Myrtle District Library. Everything about her clashed with the man she was talking to, from her dress to her tinkly little-girl laugh — it should have sounded like an air horn coming from that bosom — to the half-eaten doughnut in the paper napkin in her right hand, covered with pink and white sprinkles. Laurie wondered, if she were to tell the woman who and what she was talking to, whether she'd go on eating the doughnut.

Directly across from Benjamin — employees had removed several book racks and tables to make room for the paying customers to line up later, and Laurie could have stretched a measuring tape in a diagonal between them — stood Kevin, the security man, with his hands at his sides and not even a token glass in either of them. The attitude discouraged attempts to approach him or begin a conversation. Most of his weight seemed to be on his right leg, and Laurie guessed he was left-handed. At Toledo Medical she'd treated police officers whose partners stood outside the examining room favoring the leg opposite the hip their sidearms were on, an old habit and probably one they were no longer aware of. She supposed it gave them leverage to draw, if "draw" was the word they used. She'd have to ask Peter about that.

She looked back at Peter then, and it occurred to her that she could have stretched the same measuring tape from him to the guard and gotten the same straight line. The three men occupied points of a triangle, with most of the bookstore inside it and equally unobstructed views of both doors that led in from outside. She looked again at Benjamin, and back at Peter, and had to juggle her glass to keep from dropping it. Each of them was leaning on one leg, and had been for as long as she'd been watching them.

"What do you think's the capacity in a store that size?" McCormick asked. "Wonder if they're in violation."

"That's the fire marshal's worry. He's probably inside. The police chief's the only official that isn't." Prine glowered at the mass of bodies stirring on the other side of the display windows. They were sitting in his unmarked car, parked next to the space where a sign belonging to the nearby pharmacy asked patrons to leave their carts. There were two carts inside it, and half a dozen more spotted around the lot, one blocking a handicapped space.

"I asked him about that. He said he doesn't read books."

"He's read his share of menus."

"I've seen fatter."

Prine unhooked his mike and checked around. Everyone, city and state, was in place.

McCormick said, "If there's a hit-and-run downtown, they'll have to call the Cub Scouts. You sure Grinnell's in there? He went to his bank this morning. He could be in Florida."

"Macklin's in there. That's his car." He looked from it to his lieutenant. "Where's your vest?"

"Where's yours?"

"I never got around to having a new one made after I outgrew the last one. I can't get my size off the rack."

"You don't wear one, *I* don't wear one." McCormick scratched his head, dislodging some cut hairs. Every time his wife gave him a haircut, Prine had to have the car vacuumed out. It was like driving around with a sheepdog. "You sure we shouldn't hit 'em on the way in? That's a lot of hostages."

"First sign of riot gear and they drive right on past. We'll just have to do this all over again. Anyway, there won't be so many when they show up. They don't go in until just before closing."

"It's their first bookstore. Maybe they changed that part too."

"You don't rob a place until there's cash in the registers."

McCormick hesitated. "I forgot about that."

Prine snapped his Desert Eagle out of its underarm clip and racked a shell into the chamber, breaking one of his own regulations. He hadn't been in the field in years and wasn't sure of his reflexes under fire. "That's why I hired you, Mac. You don't think like a criminal."

"I love you." The speaker's voice throbbed.

"Don't say that." Same voice, roughened a little.

"Why not? It's true." Throb.

"That's even worse. Whenever you fall in love, with whoever you fall in love with, the ending can't be happy. Someone winds up alone." Rough.

"Someone winds up alone either way."

"What *is* this shit?" Mark Twain demanded from the backseat.

Wild Bill half turned in the front passenger's seat and tossed the box into Mark's lap. *Serpent in Eden* landed with the pictures of the author and movie-star reader on top. "I told Donny to boost a van with a tape deck. You ever listen to books on tape?"

"I didn't even read the one with me in it. Find a rap station."

"I thought everybody liked Matt Damon."

"Who the fuck's he?"

Wild Bill turned off the tape deck. "My little redhead says Spain moved a thousand copies in Buffalo last week. I guess there's something we ain't hearing."

"I fucked a redhead once," Mark said. "Never again. You get their clothes off, they look like a skinned squirrel. I never felt so black."

"All we had was coffee and doughnuts. She sure liked to talk, even when her mouth was full. I had one Marjorie every place we hit, we wouldn't've needed Grinnell."

"Now you're starting to sound like Carlos."

"Poor Carlos. I don't miss him."

"Why'd you shoot him?" Donny asked.

"Why not shoot Carlos?" Mark said. "He was born to be shot."

"I mean before the bookstore. It's a big job for just two inside."

"Mark and me'll just work harder by half."

"What about that rap station?" Mark asked.

"I want to get barked at by some colored guys, I'll drive up to Detroit, put a ding in a Lincoln Continental. You tell me you listen to that shit at home, put your sock feet up on a Barcalounger and turn on Old Dirty Bastard, you're a liar. That's just for cruising the suburbs, piss off the soccer moms driving their giant SUVs."

"You got to be in a mood for it."

"Anything sounds good on parrot pills. DPW guys busting up a sidewalk."

"You ever try listening to Toby Keith without a six-pack of Bud? It's all the same world, man."

"Lay off Toby. He put the western back in country and western. The women just about made off with it before he came along."

"Fucking sellout. You never saw Tupac banging no guitar with *Ford* plastered all over it."

"Maybe they never asked him. He took two in the belly before they got around to it." Wild Bill was having fun. It was always like this before they hit a place, all of them wired up tight as a bale of hay. It was better without Carlos and his Baby Ruths and his bullshit Mafia stories. Having to stop every ten blocks to use the toilet.

Donny said, "There's Olive Garden. Pasta's quick energy."

"A little Dago Red go good about now," Mark said. "I'm out of pills."

“One glass,” Wild Bill said, “you go right to sleep.”

“I’ll spit out half.”

Donny wheeled the big Econoline into the restaurant parking lot. All the spaces were taken. People were sitting and leaning on the railing outside the building.

Wild Bill said, “Keep driving. I wanted to stand in line to eat I’d join the army.”

Mark said, “Mexican’s good. Raise a margarita to old Carlos.”

“Good idea. That way if a cash register’s locked, you can blow it open with a fart.” Wild Bill leaned forward and switched the sound system back on. Matt Damon put the throb in his voice.

“Why is it so hard for you to admit you care about anyone besides yourself?”

“Who said I care for myself?”

“Oh, shit,” Mark said. “Find a pet store.”

TWENTY-FIVE

In her four years on the labor market — in the course of which she had drawn paychecks from seventeen different employers — Marjorie Chesswick had never worked so hard in one day, at a job so monotonous.

She had come close during the three weeks she'd spent in the back room of a community shopper in Chillicothe, folding and stuffing advertising supplements into five thousand copies of *The Ross County Consumer* (the publishers claimed a circulation of twenty-five thousand, on the theory that each one was read by an average of five people), and it had been filthy work besides, smearing her hands and face and clothes with several shades of smelly ink, but at least there she'd been one of three employees working side by side, and the time had passed quickly in conversation and laughter. On this job, she was dealing directly with customers, unable to visit with the other slaves without appearing rude, and she couldn't encourage discourse with the people across the counter without slowing up the line. Pamela was adamant about not keeping patrons waiting.

Marjorie thought she would've enjoyed the cocktail party that preceded the signing — getting to meet the guest of honor, drinking champagne and discussing books with the president of the village council and the branch manager of the bank — but Pamela had invited only Caroline, her senior cashier, for that, from among the staff. The rest had been told to show up thirty minutes before the doors opened, to clear away the glasses and crumbs and napkins and unlock the registers. By then most of the VIPs had left, and Spain was busy inscribing books purchased earlier by long-time customers who couldn't attend the signing. Once when he raised his head, Marjorie had smiled at him, but he'd looked right past her to ask Pamela for a pitcher of water and a glass, instead of the plastic squirt bottle she'd provided. Apparently big-time authors flew too high above the ground to drink distilled water or take notice of the help.

When she'd applied for the job, she'd imagined working in a bookstore was a genteel experience, sitting on a stool behind the counter reading, sipping tea brewed from the contents of the elegant foil-wrapped packages displayed in the giftware section and marking her place with a finger while she completed the odd transaction; talking about T. S. Eliot and Maya Angelou with her fellow workers after closing. She had a BA in English Literature and until she had enough put by to go for her MA and a teaching certificate, it would have been the closest she came to using her education since commencement.

She'd spent her first day climbing up and down a stepladder in the back room, stacking remainders and countless heavy cartons on shelves, and getting paper cuts from the lacerated jackets of Hurt Books as she applied red discount stickers to them. It was sweaty and achy, and nearly as filthy as stuffing newspapers. Even new books shed sooty dust and bits of Styrofoam packing material that clung stubbornly to her fingers when she tried to flick them off. Her fellow workers didn't know Maya Angelou from Miss Piggy, and even the customers left the foil-wrapped bricks of tea on the shelves. In eight months on the job she hadn't sold one.

But stripping was the most disheartening work of all. No one who admired books and loved reading could spend an afternoon ripping the covers off unsold paperbacks to return to the publishers and dumping their nude carcasses into a big plastic trash can. That was the closest thing to the one ghastly day she'd worked for the humane society, watching cages of puppies and kittens being carried out to the gasworks behind the kennels.

She'd made up her mind to quit right after the Francis Spain signing. She'd have given notice sooner, but she wanted to meet her first real live author, and she couldn't leave Pamela and the others shorthanded so close to the big event. In fact, she'd just come to that decision when a Kentucky cowboy had approached the counter with a smile and conversation that said she was more than a machine hooked up to a cash register, and later an invitation to sit down over coffee and Krispy Kremes and share the details of their lives. He'd been a fishing guide in Montana, had hunted all over the West, and had come back home to claim an inheritance and figure out what to do with the rest of his life. So they were in the same situation, not counting the inheritance.

She liked his long clean hair, his moustache like corn silk, his Southern accent with its frontier overlay, and his kind eyes, which looked brown or green depending on the light — *hazel*, she thought it was called. He wasn't much older than she, certainly not thirty, but his face was weathered from exposure and there was a kind of sadness about him that supported his determination to change directions. His friends called him Wild Bill, he'd said, but he wasn't feeling so wild these days. She'd told him some things as well, mostly about the bookstore and how it operated, things about Pamela. He'd said he was thinking of going into the book business, opening a store of his own. She'd told him it was no work for anyone who liked books. He'd said that was no problem, he preferred movies, especially westerns. She didn't think she'd ever seen a western, but on his recommendation she'd stopped at a video store on her way back to work and rented *Tombstone*. Val Kilmer had reminded her a little of Bill, beautiful and sad.

It was the best part of the last eight months; but it was only an hour, one lunch break out of 160. He hadn't said anything about asking her out again. Probably he was repelled by her red hair and freckles. Men liked them at first sight, but they got old fast. She wished her grandmother had come from Sweden instead of County Limerick. So that was that. She didn't even know his last name.

This today was just plain soul-destroying. She kept looking at the same damn book with the same damn cover, seasoned occasionally with an impulse item — *Love Song* in paperback, mostly, or a decorative bookmark — but not very often. You got tired of looking at it, scanning the code, skidding the book across the magnetized counter to deactivate the antitheft device, and stuffing it in the bag with the receipt, over and over. "Thank you. I can help the next person in line." It was like working in a factory and a long way from the literary experience she'd expected.

"Smile. You got forty years till retirement."

She looked up from the current copy of *Serpent in Eden* to the face of the customer who had put it in front of her. Bill was smiling at her from under the lank moustache. He wore a jean jacket buttoned to the neck.

Her cheeks cracked. She realized she was smiling back. Grinning. "Hello! I didn't think you were coming back."

"I said I was. I almost didn't when I saw the line. Then I remembered there was someone I wanted to buy the book for."

He pried it out of her professional grip, opened it to the title page, and spun it around on the counter. It was signed: *To Marjorie. Best, Francis Spain.*

"You didn't go ahead and buy it?" He sounded anxious.

"No. I wanted to. I have an employee discount, but I owe rent and I don't get paid till next week. Are you sure you want to give it to me? It's an expensive book."

"I wouldn't've stood in line for an hour if I didn't. I listened to some of it on tape. It's all right, I guess. I think I told you I don't read much."

"You're just not reading the right kind of books for you." She glanced over toward Spain and saw Pamela watching her. "I'll put this in a bag and give it to you. You can give it to me later, if you still want."

"When's closing?"

The line had dwindled to a few dozen people, mostly middle-aged women. "Fifteen minutes by the clock, but I doubt we'll turn anyone away. It'll take about an hour to finish up." She took his cash, gave him change and the bag with the book in it. She smiled. "Thank you. No man's ever given me a book."

His smile was sad. "See you in an hour."

* * *

McCormick looked at his watch, a Seiko. "They ought to be closing up about now."

"There are still people waiting," Prine said.

"They'll go in before the doors are locked. Blasting your way in spoils the surprise."

Prine watched a leggy cowboy type in a jean jacket stride across the parking lot, carrying a store bag. He kept on walking and disappeared around the corner of the health club. Not a few of the patrons had come in on foot. There were several new subdivisions within walking distance. "I'll pull in the unmarkeds. I don't want this crew circling the block, counting SWAT teams." He unhooked the mike.

When he signed off, McCormick said, "No sign of Macklin. Maybe he went out the back."

"He's still inside."

"You see him?"

"No, but I can see Grinnell. Neither one of these bums is going to walk out and leave the other with the candy."

It got quiet in the car.

"You think it was Macklin cooled the guy in the music shop?" McCormick asked.

"I hope so. The state's not big enough for two like him."

"Means he's got a gun."

"We've got more."

Macklin asked Laurie what she thought of Spain. They were standing by the magazine rack, out of the writer's earshot. Spain never looked up from the books he was signing to see who he was signing them for.

"I'm not disappointed." She sounded tense.

He looked across at Grinnell, who was pretending interest in the computer books. The man remained in full view of the windows and the security guard.

"What's going to happen?" Laurie asked.

"Your mother's going to make Employee of the Month."

Her face was unreadable. "You promised me no more secrets."

"I don't know any more than you do."

"You're armed. So is Benjamin."

That surprised him — not that Grinnell was carrying, but that she knew it. He nodded. "I'm armed because he is."

"You couldn't have known that when you were getting ready to come here."

"I guessed it."

"What did he tell you that night that you aren't telling me?"

"Not a thing. That's the truth."

"I want all the truth. Not just some of it."

"So do I. He's got something in mind, and I think it's for tonight. But I don't know what it is."

"Does it have to do with Spain?"

"I don't know what it would be if it does."

"Why don't I go up and ask him?"

"No."

"I said why don't I?"

He said nothing.

"You son of a bitch." She turned Grinnell's way, dress rustling.

Macklin's hand shot out and closed on her wrist. She spun back in his direction, face twisted. He put his face close to hers and dropped his voice almost to a whisper.

"Because if you go near him, it'll be like he's got *two* guns pointed at me."

The tension went out of her after a moment. He let go of her wrist. The imprint of his fingers showed on the skin, but she didn't rub it. "You're still a son of a bitch," she said. "And if you're alive after tonight, I want a divorce."

* * *

Mark Twain drew the book out of the bag and turned it toward the streetlight. They were parked at a meter three blocks from the bookstore. The village didn't collect from meters after six o'clock.

"Jesus. You want to fuck this guy or what? You keep buying the same book."

"It's a gift." Wild Bill slung an arm across the back of the front seat and snatched back the book. Mark had grabbed it from him as he was getting in. "They'll be tied up another hour. We're not waiting that long."

"You was *gone* a hour. We thought you was busted."

"I didn't," Donny said.

"It ain't you'd be doing this job solo if he was, so shut the fuck up."

Wild Bill felt sad. Mark was starting to get unreliable without the pills. It was the first break in their little family; Carlos had been an outsider, forced on them by Toledo. Tonight was definitely the end. "Security's a big guy in a blue blazer, no eyebrows. Standing fifteen feet in from the door, to the left. Didn't budge all the time I was there."

"What about Grinnell?"

"He's in there, Macklin too. Same plan as before."

"What plan?" Donny asked.

"You just drive," Mark said. "Let us worry about what's inside."

Wild Bill said, "There's some heavy weight inside. There'll be shooting."

"That ain't his lookout. Why stir him up?"

"He'll hear the shots." Wild Bill reached over and gripped Donny's thigh. "This won't be Hilliard. This time we know what's coming."

Donny stared at the windshield. "A hit is what it sounds like."

"A hit's when you walk into a restaurant and put two in somebody's head," Wild Bill said. "This is nothing like that."

"What's it like?"

"Hunting." He shrugged out of his jean jacket, exposing his red shirt, and stuck his hand out at Mark for the shotgun.

TWENTY-SIX

It was one of the strangest moments in Grinnell's generally unorthodox Ohio experience.

When Wild Bill came in the door, they'd locked eyes briefly, but from then on Grinnell might have been one of the books on the shelves for all the attention the young desperado paid him. Wild Bill took his place at the end of the line of empty souls waiting for their ten seconds with a celebrity who couldn't be bothered to look up and see who was keeping him independent of honest work. When his turn came he told Spain what he wanted him to write — Grinnell was standing too far away to make it out — and stood silent while Pamela took a book off the stack and opened it to the title page and held it for the famous pen. Wild Bill thanked the author and joined the line at checkout.

Grinnell wasn't surprised by the visit. He knew the crew wanted to know what the security guard looked like, and Wild

Bill's interest in Macklin was such that he'd need an idea of Macklin's position before they came through the door. Having a book signed and paying for it would prevent anyone from taking special notice of him. What was strange about the whole thing was it was the first time Grinnell and Wild Bill had been on the scene of a robbery at the same time. A case man had no more direct part in such a business than an accountant had with the actual exchange of cash whose figures he entered in his columns. He was a little surprised that his pulse wasn't more rapid. Tommy Vulpo would have been astounded. But Tommy Vulpo knew very little about Grinnell.

In fact he'd felt calmer than he had in weeks. He'd felt that way since the moment he'd decided to visit his bank and take out his discretionary fund — case dough, Toledo would call it. He wouldn't miss the organization in Toledo, but he was a little sorry to leave behind his comfortable condominium with its view of the lake and its handy hiding place for contraband on the other side of the common wall he shared with his neighbor. He already missed his Lexus. He had nothing against American-made cars — had in fact been most disappointed with the Mercedes he'd owned for a few months in the early nineties — but given the luxury of time he'd have opted for a Lincoln or a Cadillac or even a Chrysler Town Car before driving the bare-bones Ford he'd parked behind the store. His middle-aged frame retained a sense-memory of every fissure and pothole he'd encountered since Mason.

He owed Pamela one more act of protection. Difficult, self-involved, and too critical of those close to her, she nevertheless had a way of making him feel safe when they were together. She was the perfect blind. She accepted his studied dullness with the faith of a convert, reinforced it in the presence of others, and after her husband's betrayal was so determined to succeed on her own that the lack of competition from her mate attracted her in ways that mere male beauty could not. She trusted him, and he wouldn't find that again, wherever he ended up. But he'd been too long in one place.

After Wild Bill left with his purchase, Grinnell went to the employee rest room in the shipping and storage area. He had to walk around a stepladder to open the door. The room was cluttered with racks and books that had been removed from the shop to ease congestion, and someone had shoved aside the ladder to make room. He splashed water on his face and inspected the magazine in the handle of the Browning BDA yet again.

The door bumped against the stepladder when he came out, and like most people faced with the obstacle of a ladder looked up to the top. A rectangular panel was set in the ceiling with a pull-ring attached, probably to give plumbers and electricians access to the equipment above. He hadn't noticed it before.

Laurie suddenly hated being a woman, and hated even more being a woman men found attractive.

Hated the way the black cocktail dress showed off her well-shaped collarbone and long legs, hated her sapphire earrings — a six-month anniversary present from Peter — hated the way they brought out the startling blue in her eyes, hated, hated, hated. She wished she were a lesbian, one of the obvious types who wore frumpy sweaters with cat hair on them, baggy cargo pants and Birkenstocks and her hair in a greasy bun. Her luck with women would have had to be better than her luck with men. All the men in her life — her philandering father, her mother's sinister boyfriend, the man she'd pledged the rest of her days to — had played her false. Well, her grandfather hadn't, but maybe he'd been just too old to take the trouble. Maybe his past behavior had been the reason for her grandmother's chronic irritability.

For Peter she'd turned her back on her own principles, agreed to accept his vile past in return for a promise of honesty — accompliced herself to the act of murder for it — and he'd spat it back in her face. Her mother had been right all along: A man was a man. You couldn't adopt a massasauga rattler and feed it warm milk and expect it to curl up in your lap, purr, and not be a snake.

Something hideous was going to happen that night, right there in her mother's world, and Laurie had brought it. She didn't know what it was, whether Peter and Benjamin were going head to head or standing shoulder to shoulder, but blood was going to flow. She'd suspected it ever since the night Peter had told her that Benjamin was a player, and yet she'd gone right on dreaming about living on a farm, like some kind of postnuclear Heidi. It made her want to rip off her dress and claw herself until she bled. Instead she pushed through the line standing in front of Spain's table, forcing a collective grunt from tired customers who thought she was cutting in, and walked around the table to stand beside her mother.

"I need to talk to you," Laurie said.

"In a few minutes, dear. Francis is almost finished." Pamela slid a book off the top of the stack. They were close to selling out.

"It's about Benjamin."

Pamela turned toward her, but her eyes went past her daughter, toward the front door. The vertical line between her brows deepened. Laurie turned that way. Two men in red shirts and black ski masks were coming in. The one in front carried a short shotgun.

"It's going down! Move in! Now! Now!" Humiliatingly, Prine's voice cracked. The microphone felt clumsy in his hand.

The big Econoline van had come wailing around the end of the strip and disgorged its payload of armed passengers before it came to a complete stop. The front door of the bookstore drifted shut behind them. Then from inside came two sharp cracks, followed by the concussion of a shotgun. Prine shoved down the door handle on his side. McCormick already had a foot on the pavement, reaching behind his hip for his deep-bellied Ruger. He wasn't as far away from active duty as his superior, and his reflexes showed it.

Blue-and-red strobes and sirens filled the parking lot. Prine had on his hip-length blue jacket with POLICE across the back in reflective yellow letters eight inches high, but as he unclipped the Desert Eagle he stuck his shield up above his head to catch the searchlights. He was just wondering if Mac, in civilian clothes, had thought to do the same thing when a bullhorn voice bawled, "Police! Drop your weapon!" and he saw his lieutenant turn with the Ruger in his fist and topple backward in a rattle of gunfire.

Wild Bill took a side step inside the door, giving Mark a clear field of fire. Mark located the bodyguard where Wild Bill had said he'd be and shot him twice as he was unharnessing a big semiautomatic pistol. Wild Bill looked for Grinnell in his spot, found the spot empty, and lost a beat that nearly cost him his head, because Macklin threw down on him with a revolver. But just then one of the customers who'd been in line zigged into his line of fire and he held off. The shotgun whammed, pushing against Wild Bill's hip, and a shelf of books fell apart; Macklin had flung himself to the floor. Wild Bill tried to follow him down with the shotgun, but lost sight of him in the scatter of bodies, the copies of *Serpent in Eden* arcing this way and that in midair, jettisoned for flight.

Sirens howled outside. Shots crackled. So Grinnell had made a call. There went Donny, along with their ride.

The boss lady was Mark's second target — payoff for Grinnell's waffling — but Wild Bill was too busy looking for Macklin and Grinnell to see where Mark's shots were landing. The money had no meaning now. No matter what kind of plan you made, it all went to hell the first time someone fired a gun. But he glanced toward the counter, just in case Grinnell had been crouching behind it, and his eyes locked with Marjorie's — redheaded Marjorie, with the big freckles — frozen in the act of shoving a book into a plastic bag. He thought he saw recognition there. All the women he'd ever been friendly with had had something to say about his eyes. No Grinnell there.

Something cracked past his left ear, a tiny sonic boom. It whacked the door frame. He whirled toward its source, swinging the shotgun to shoulder level, and there was Francis Spain, the celebrity author, grinning at him. (Grinning?) Wild Bill squeezed the trigger and blew his head off.

Macklin saw Kevin, the security guard, drawing, too late for the man standing fifteen feet away with his Sig Sauer already in hand, but although he'd drawn the Dan Wesson the instant he'd seen movement through the glass of the front door, he picked the man with the shotgun instead, because Laurie and her mother were standing in his line of fire and he had to draw him off. Kevin stumbled backward, struck twice by bullets from the Sig, and then a panicking customer crossed right in front of Macklin and he had to dive as the shotgun's blast walloped the air just above his head. The floor came up hard; he landed on his gun arm and almost lost his grip on the revolver, but he came up on his knees still holding it, found the shotgunner looking away from him, toward the counter, and snapped off a shot that missed because his arm was numb and he couldn't feel the trigger. Then he had to roll again as the shotgun came up and exploded a second time.

He struck something with his shoulder and something else, a lot of somethings, rained down on him, bouncing off his head and chest, copies of *Serpent in Eden*, dislodged from the autograph table when he rolled into it. He looked up, saw Laurie's black skirt, seized one of her trim ankles, and jerked it out from under her. She fell on top of him in a pile. She screamed something and shoved at him with her hand, trying to push herself up, but he threw his free arm around her waist and held on. He heard what she was screaming then. "Mother!"

There was no sign of Spain. Pamela was still standing in her original spot, just standing there while everyone else was scrambling for cover, holding a copy of Spain's book open to the title page, the table at her feet, staring down at Laurie and Macklin in a tangle on the floor beside it. Macklin straightened his other arm and pointed the revolver up at his mother-in-law. "Get down."

Literally blew his head off. Wild Bill stared at the ragged top of Spain's neck, bits of stuff floating down all around, watched the rest of his body teeter and flop over backward like a board, books spilling from his middle, and lie on the floor as flat as a cartoon rabbit run over by a steam-roller. Then he turned a little and saw Spain again, standing ten feet in front of him still wearing his head. Half of it was hidden behind a tall, good-looking young woman in a business suit. He was crouching.

Wild Bill laughed. He didn't know if he was laughing at the sissy book writer hiding behind a woman's skirts or at him-self for wasting a shell on a cardboard cutout.

The woman's face was all white and eyes. "Please don't shoot me." She had a New York accent.

He stopped laughing. Fiber from the ski mask had gotten into his mouth. He snatched it off and threw it away. Then he continued his search for Macklin and Grinnell, in that order. He was pretty sure now Grinnell had lit out the back when he and Mark had come in. Case men were all pussies when the shooting started. He'd lost track of Mark.

"Police! Put down the weapon and throw up your hands!"

Someone bumped him, trying to get out of the way. He let go of the shotgun with one hand, grabbed a fistful of hair, and spun into the body. When he had it against him he realized the hair was red and recognized Marjorie's gingery perfume. Everything about her reminded him of doughnuts. The cop standing inside the front door hesitated. Wild Bill fired. The cop was wearing riot gear, helmet and face shield and shin guards, and probably a vest, but the blast carried him back through the door, his own shotgun firing wide and obliterating a display of self-help guides.

The display windows were filling with uniforms. Wild Bill backpedaled, taking Marjorie with him. He tripped and fell on his ass, losing his grip on his hostage. She whimpered and fled. He rolled onto his shoulder and looked at Mark, the thing he'd stumbled over, eyes sightless in the holes in his mask.

Wild Bill flopped onto his stomach, rested the shotgun across Mark's belly, and using the body as a breastwork swiveled the barrel slowly from side to side, his eyes moving with it. He spotted movement and saw Macklin rising from the floor a dozen feet away, rising up and up until he was as tall as a mountain, the revolver in his hand. Wild Bill tightened his finger on the trigger.

A block of cement hit him square between the shoulders. The wind gusted out of his lungs and he knew he'd been shot, but he was all animal instinct now, a wounded bull elk with the river at its back, and he rolled over, swinging the shotgun straight up, toward Benjamin Grinnell, Grinnell framed from the waist up in a square hole in the ceiling pointing a pistol down at him. Wild Bill thought he heard his shotgun roar. He never found out for sure.

TWENTY-SEVEN

"I never saw so many shotgun rounds fired with so little to show for it."

Edgar Prine looked at the Myrtle police chief, a short fat man in a russet sport coat who looked like the owner of an appliance store, which he probably was.

"I've got a man in Emergency with a collapsed lung and my second in command's on a table having a kidney removed. How much show do you like?"

"Your lieutenant was unavoidable. He turned a gun on my officers and he didn't identify himself."

Prine said nothing. His mistake was in bringing in the locals to begin with. He'd long suspected Hoover had been right about that and now his suspicions were confirmed. Mac's face had been ghastly pale when they were rolling him into the EMS van, like carved soap. That was one picture he'd have a long time. To his grave, if Mac didn't pull through.

He looked down at Grinnell, paler yet as

the ME's men worked the zipper up the Mylar bag toward his face. Theory was he'd climbed up into the suspended ceiling in the back room, lifted out one of the frosted glass panels when he'd reached the shop, and plucked off the black perpetrator from above, just like shooting fish in a bucket. But he'd missed the other one's vitals and paid for it with a load of double-O buck in the chest. He'd fired simultaneously with the shotgunner, put one through the brain on the second try. Not too shabby for the mob equivalent of a file clerk.

He wondered why he'd bothered. He knew he'd been burned, had shaken a good man and could have kept on driving, but he'd stepped right back into the fire. Prine looked over at Grinnell's woman, the bookstore manager, talking animatedly with her hands to the officer scribbling in his notebook: good-enough looking for a woman in her middle years, but even from this distance she looked like a pain in someone's ass. There was no accounting for taste, particularly when it involved a criminal.

Anyway, that was the cost of three trials spared the People of the State of Ohio — four, counting the one at the motel in

Harbor View. The wheelman had surrendered without resistance, and unless Prine applied leverage, the prosecutor's office would probably let him deal himself out of Felony Murder with a plea to Robbery Armed. He'd see how he felt about that after he spoke to Mac's surgeons.

He walked away from the chief without excusing himself and approached the group of state police interviewing the manager's daughter, Macklin's wife. Another group had gathered around the cashier who'd been taken hostage, rocking back and forth on a straight chair with someone's uniform jacket draped across her shoulders. He'd been in service long enough to see psychiatric counseling become part of police work. She'd been in the perp's clutches thirty seconds.

"Mrs. Macklin, my name is Captain Prine. I'm in charge of the State Police Armed Robbery Task Force."

"Yes, I've seen you on TV."

He watched her closely. She seemed icily calm, and he didn't know yet if it was shock or the standard pickled-in-brine attitude of the career mob wife. She was a pretty thing, with an athletic body in a short black dress. She didn't look at all like a tart.

"Your husband's in custody. His time will be easier if he cooperates with our investigation. Can you tell me what part he played in what happened tonight?"

"He was an invited guest at Mr. Spain's autograph party."

"Some people think he was a bit more. He was seen shooting at one of the robbers."

"Someone's mixed up. My husband is retired from the retail camera business. He's never shot anything more than a picture."

He knew what she was then. A tart was a tart in a designer dress or shorts and a halter. He put an edge in his voice.

"We've recovered a revolver, a thirty-eight caliber. One of the robbers had a shotgun and the other was armed with a semiautomatic pistol. Grin— Mr. Grinnell, your mother's, ah, gentleman friend, had a semiautomatic. The revolver is the only weapon unaccounted for. Does your husband own a gun?"

"No."

"You realize even if he wiped off his fingerprints before he abandoned it, we'll be able to tell if he fired a gun recently."

"I know that. I told you I watch TV."

"You realize it's against the law to lie to a

police officer? Your husband may not be the only one who's in trouble."

"I'm pretty sure everyone in this country has a right to lie to anyone, as long as it's not under oath. But I'm telling you the truth, Captain. May I ask where you've taken my husband? I need to notify our lawyer."

"He'll be able to call him in person. I'm sure he knows that, if the officers forget to tell him. Your husband's a bad man, Mrs. Macklin. A gangster and a professional killer and I don't know what else."

"I thought your interest was armed robbery."

One of the officers coughed into a fist. Prine thought he was covering a chuckle. He made a mental note of the name on his tag. "Maybe your mother can give me more information."

"Don't be too hard on her. She's had a long day."

Her concern seemed genuine. He wasn't sure what to make of her.

"Ms. Ziegenthaler?"

"Mrs.," the manager corrected. "My daughter's legitimate. You're Edgar Prine, aren't you? Was this the Color Guard?"

He studied her pupils. She didn't appear to be in shock. "I'm sorry about Mr.

Grinnell. I don't normally condone private citizens taking the law into their own hands, but he died courageously."

"It was a surprise, I can tell you. I haven't taken it in yet. If you ever met Benjamin, you'd have forgotten him five minutes later. He was a good man, but very ordinary. I'm afraid it's my fault, what he did. He was showing off for me."

She spoke rapidly, using her hands. He wouldn't want to be near her when the adrenaline ran out. She reminded him of everyone's ex-wife he'd ever met. For a moment he felt sorry for Ben Grinnell.

That didn't last. He believed that criminals comprised a subhuman species, produced from a polluted gene pool. The practical thing to do was exterminate them, like euthanizing diseased cattle; but years of lobbying on his part had failed to overturn the state ban on the death penalty.

"Actually, I did meet him once," he said. "But I wanted to ask you about the gun. Had you ever seen it before?"

"Would you happen to have a cigarette, Captain? These officers all live too healthy."

"Sorry. I gave them up years ago."

"So did I. I didn't see the gun tonight,

let alone any other time. I was on the floor with my daughter and son-in-law and didn't get up until the shooting was over."

"You were on the floor with your son-in-law?"

"And my daughter. He pulled me down. A very practical young man. Not so young, actually; he could be Laurie's father. No foolish hero like — well, poor Benjamin. He was selfish at the end."

"Macklin?"

"Benjamin. I suppose he saved some lives, but what will I do now?" Her chin trembled. It was the first crack in the dam, and Prine's cue to put distance between them. But he pressed on.

"Macklin had a gun, too. He fired it at least once."

"Who told you that?" She looked interested.

"We have a room full of eyewitnesses."

"Oh, witnesses. Everyone *I* saw was running for their lives. Someone's got it all turned around, Captain. Peter wouldn't have the imagination for such a thing. He's exactly the kind of man you always hope your daughter will marry. Prosperous and boring."

"You said the same thing about Benjamin."

Her forehead creased. He thought she was about to cry. "Do you know where Mr. Spain went?" she asked then. "I saw him and Miss Jacobetti in a crowd of policemen, but I didn't get to talk to them. I'm going to report Heartland Protection to the regional manager. God rest that poor man's soul, but he was certainly slow on the uptake when push came to shove."

Prine's jaw clenched until it creaked. The man had been an air marshal, a member of the law-enforcement community. The black man had shot him as if he were a road sign. "It's a bodyguard's duty to put his client's life before his own. He did what he was hired to do."

"Yes, yes. But what about Mr. Spain?"

"He's at Toledo Express Airport, waiting for a flight. I put him and his publicist in the backseat of a state police unit personally."

"Like common criminals."

"All the common criminals in this case are dead," he snapped. "Or in custody."

She bent and brushed dust off the hem of her skirt. "Well, I don't suppose he'd have come back anyway." She looked up. "You have the experience in these things. Do you think it would be appropriate if I sent him a basket of some kind?"

Someone touched his arm. He looked at a tired trooper with his hair plastered to his forehead with sweat. He had his helmet under one arm.

"Captain, I've been interviewing the female hostage. She knew the man who grabbed her."

"Thank you, Miss Chesswick. These officers will take you home." He smiled down at the redheaded cashier, who nodded without looking up. She looked tiny with a trooper's coat across her shoulders.

Wild Bill. He shook his head and rejoined the police chief, who told him he had an unmarked unit waiting at the back door.

"I didn't think you wanted to talk to the press yet," the chief said. "They're crawling all over the parking lot."

Prine thanked him, and in the act moved the chief several notches up on his personal list. He gave him the card containing his business and home numbers and went out through the cluttered storage room. A city officer was waiting beside a gray Chrysler. He saluted smartly, impressing the captain, and opened the door to the backseat.

“Where can I take you, sir?”

“Mercy Hospital.” He put a foot inside.

“Captain Prine!”

He looked past the officer. A young woman he hadn’t seen stepped forward from the Dumpster behind the bookstore. Her hair, cut in bangs to her eyebrows, was dyed deep cranberry and she had more metal in her face than the car he was climbing into. A laminated press card dangled from a clothespin clamped to the neck of her green tank top. Her bare arms were purple with tattoos. He looked at the officer, who stepped between her and Prine.

“No comment. I’ll announce a press conference tomorrow.” He sank back into the upholstery.

“I don’t want to ask any questions — yet. I wanted to thank you for the police credentials.” She craned her neck to smile at him over the officer’s shoulder, holding up the card and waggling it. Prine saw the state seal.

He made a backhand wave. The officer frowned and stepped aside.

“What’s your name?” He studied the young woman, who looked as if she belonged behind the counter of a coffee shop. He was sure they’d never met.

“Tasha Wilkes. I’m with the *Bowling*

Green Blast. Actually, I *am* the *Blast.* Me and PageMaker."

A tired smile tugged at the corners of his mouth. " 'Hue Crew Screws Blues.' "

Her cheeks colored, an interesting contrast with all that steel. "I wrote that. I write everything, including the advertisements, when I can get them. I built the Web site, too. I'm majoring in Journalism and Computer Design."

"Minoring in Breaking and Entering?"

"Oh, Officer Alfiero told you about the music store. I wasn't breaking in. I tried the doorknob to see if it was locked." The smile evaporated. "I'm sorry about Lieutenant McCormick. I heard about it on the scanner."

"Thank you." He suppressed a sigh. Girl reporters and lady cops; the order of the universe was in serious disarray. "Where do you stand on convict rehabilitation?"

Her face went flat. "I'm not the one to ask."

"Why not?"

"My sister was raped and beaten by a man twelve hours after he was released from a three-year sentence for rape. I think violent felons should be locked up for life."

He slid over and patted the vacant seat. "Get in."

TWENTY-EIGHT

George Tiplady had fought very hard for the corner office after Phil Forrestal retired. During the fight he'd blackened the reputations of two other attorneys with several years' seniority over him and earned their enmity for life, but it had been worth it. He himself didn't care about the view it offered of sparkling Lake Erie and the skyscrapers of downtown Toledo, but the subliminal promise of freedom that came with it had landed him some fabulous clients, mostly women whose husbands could be depended upon to pay all his fees and court costs when the divorce papers came through.

At age thirty-four, Tiplady was the youngest partner in the firm of Voorhaven, Forrestal, and Steeb, with a parking spot two down from old Grover Voorhaven's and a thirty-foot cabin cruiser berthed at the Maumee Yacht Club named *Love on the Rocks*. He'd joined the best health club in town, lost the forty pounds of fat he'd been lugging around since high school, and spent fifteen thousand dollars on hair plugs. His was the first male face many attractive and dissatisfied women saw once they'd made the decision to leave, and the more pleasing it was, the better his chances of recruiting a topless deckhand for the weekend. *Toledo* magazine had named him one of the city's Ten Most Eligible Bachelors three years running. He was referred to as "the lady-tipper" in places where he no longer took his clients.

When his three o'clock came, he made a business of getting up, taking his jacket off the back of his chair, and shrugging into it as he came around the desk to take her hand; a quaint old-world touch he'd picked up from Voorhaven, whom no woman had seen in his shirtsleeves since Pearl Harbor. Women warmed to it, whether they noticed it on a conscious level or not, and although this one showed no reaction, he very much hoped it worked. She was the best-looking blonde he'd had in the office, elegantly dressed in a cashmere jacket over a simple white top and slacks with a razor crease. Clear-painted toenails showed through the open weave of her pumps. He was a connoisseur of female feet; women who took care of them seldom argued over expenses.

"Mrs. Macklin. I hope you won't think me disingenuous when I offer condolences."

She smiled tightly. She had a strong grip; hand weights, he guessed. Her breasts would be firm as well. "I'd like to get started."

"Of course." He showed her to the leather chair.

She declined refreshment and he sat down behind the big glass-topped desk that supported only a telephone-intercom and a green suede Levenger's pad. He asked her on what grounds she was seeking divorce.

"What've you got?"

"In this state, adultery, bigamy, separation or absence, extreme cruelty, impotency, alcohol addiction, felony conviction or imprisonment, nonsupport, insanity, mutual consent, fraud, force, and duress." He counted them off on his fingertips.

Her lips moved slightly, repeating the list. "Fraud," she said at last.

He wrote "F" on the pad. Details to come. "How long have you been married?"

"Next month will be a year."

He clucked his tongue. Three was the magic number when it came to negotiating a settlement. But he'd played the accustomed-lifestyle card successfully on as little as six weeks. "Any children?"

"No."

"Are you pregnant?"

"No."

He smiled reassuringly. "Are you sure? I can arrange a physical examination. It's best we know now."

"*I* know."

He clucked again, made a note. Then he asked the bonus question. "What does your husband do for a living?"

ABOUT THE AUTHOR

Loren D. Estleman, author of the acclaimed Amos Walker private detective novels and the Detroit series, has won four Shamus Awards from the Private Eye Writers of America, four Golden Spur Awards from the Western Writers of America, and three Western Heritage Awards from the National Cowboy Hall of Fame. He has been nominated for the Edgar Allan Poe Award, Britain's Silver Dagger Award, and the National Book Award. His other novels include the Western historical classics *Billy Gashade*, *Journey of the Dead*, and *The Master Executioner.* Detroit hit man Peter Macklin made his return in *Something Borrowed, Something Black* (2002), having previously appeared in three novels: *Kill Zone*, *Roses Are Dead*, and *Any Man's Death.* His most recent book is *Retro*, the latest Amos Walker novel. Estleman lives in Michigan with his wife, mystery author Deborah Morgan. Find out more at www.lorenestleman.com.